SAVING
CRAZY

BY THE SAME AUTHOR

Howl
The Truth About Brave

The Wild Place
Adventure Series

SAVING CRAZY

By KAREN HOOD-CADDY

DUNDURN
TORONTO

Editor: Carrie Gleason
Design: Courtney Horner
Series concept and main figure illustration by Emma Dolan
Series logo and cover design by Laura Boyle
Printer: Webcom

Library and Archives Canada Cataloguing in Publication

Hood-Caddy, Karen, 1948-, author
         Saving crazy / Karen Hood-Caddy.

(The wild place adventure series)
Issued in print and electronic formats.
ISBN 978-1-4597-3026-7

         I. Title.

PS8565.O6514S29 2015   jC813'.54   C2014-907087-X
                                                 C2014-907088-8

1   2   3   4   5   -   19   18   17   16   15

  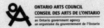

Conseil des Arts du Canada   Canada Council for the Arts

ONTARIO ARTS COUNCIL
CONSEIL DES ARTS DE L'ONTARIO
an Ontario government agency
un organisme du gouvernement de l'Ontario

We acknowledge the support of the **Canada Council for the Arts** and the **Ontario Arts Council** for our publishing program. We also acknowledge the financial support of the **Government of Canada** through the **Canada Book Fund** and **Livres Canada Books**, and the **Government of Ontario** through the **Ontario Book Publishing Tax Credit** and the **Ontario Media Development Corporation.**

Visit us at
Dundurn.com | @dundurnpress
Facebook.com/dundurnpress | Pinterest.com/dundurnpress

Dundurn
3 Church Street, Suite 500
Toronto, Ontario, Canada
M5E 1M2

To Paul Watson and his whale-saving crews.

"Those who are crazy enough to think they can change the world usually do."
— Steve Jobs

I Am Only One

I am only one,
But still I am one.
I cannot do everything,
But still I can do something;
And because I cannot do everything
I will not refuse to do the something that I can do.

— Edward Everett Hale

CHAPTER ONE

Robin sat splayed against the back seat of the van, sweat oozing out of her like the guts of a squashed fly. The air conditioner had stopped working just before they left Winnipeg and the heat made Robin feel as if she were sitting in a sauna.

Every part of her seethed with heat — her skin, her toes, even her teeth and tongue were hot. In fact, there was no part of her that wasn't hot. And there was no part of her that wasn't grumpy about it either.

Oh, what she'd give to jump into her little lake at home. She closed her eyes and imagined the feel of the wet dock under her bare feet and the moist mineral smell of the lake as she stood, readying herself to dive. In her mind, she leaned forward and plunged in, splooshing down and down into the hug of it, bubbles exploding all around her as if they were as excited as she was. The water was cool and refreshing, "invigorating" as Griff always said, and she was grateful for the way the lake pulled the blistering heat from her body. Ah, finally, relief.

She opened her eyes and wiped the sweat from her forehead with the back of her bare arm. She'd never thought she would yearn for a lake, but she was yearning for it now. Big time. As she was yearning for everything at home — Relentless, Griff, Zo-Zo — even her sister, amazingly enough. Ari was supposed to have come on the trip, but had gotten a summer job at the last moment and their dad had let her off the hook.

What was Griff doing right now, Robin wondered. Cutting away the fishing line from a duck's leg, or saving some deer that had been hit by a car? Or were she and Laura talking to some irate cottager who'd had a bear steal a salmon from their barbeque? Robin smiled. She knew she probably shouldn't root for the bears in these situations, but she couldn't help herself. Bears had to eat too, and once upon a time, all the salmon had been theirs.

Over the weeks Robin had been away, Griff had emailed a few times to say hello and give her news about what was going on at the animal shelter. Surprisingly, there hadn't been any sort of crisis. But it was August and baby season was over, so things were usually quiet at this time. That was why her dad had wanted to visit Grandpa Goodridge in Winnipeg now.

"While we're not running around like chickens with our heads cut off," he'd said.

Expecting the trip to be long, hot, and boring, both Robin and her brother, Squirm, had tried to wiggle their way out of going, but her dad had been unusually firm. Unfortunately, the trip had met all her expectations.

Robin peeled her back from the hot seat and leaned forward. "Is Grandpa Goodridge older than Griff? He acts older."

"No," her dad said. "I guess all the running around Griff does for The Wild Place keeps her young. We'll have to remind her of that the next time she tells us how tired she is."

Robin could only see his eyes in the mirror. It was funny the way eyes could smile. Just like a mouth could, but different.

"All Grandpa Goodridge does is crosswords," Squirm said.

"He bakes, too," their dad said.

Robin remembered the day they'd made peanut butter cookies. Robin had watched as her grandfather's small fingers flitted over the baking sheet like skittery birds. Griff's hands were huge and powerful and did things with calm certainty.

"Peanut butter cookies used to be your mom's favourite," Grandpa Goodridge had said.

Robin had winced at the mention of her mother. It still hurt to think of her. Would there ever come a time when she didn't react? At least nowadays she no longer cried.

Robin stuck her head out the window. The air wasn't cool, but it lifted the damp curls of her hair from her scalp and that felt good. Heat was so heavy. It was pushy too, leaning into her like a bully.

And what about Zo-Zo? What was Zo-Zo doing right now? On the Internet researching something, no doubt. At one point, Robin had tried to get her to come on the trip too, but Zo-Zo's dad had given her a summer job at his newspaper, writing articles on the environment, and Zo-Zo hadn't wanted to pass that up.

Zo-Zo had sent some of the articles to Robin, but Robin had barely been able to read them. The last one had been a list of all the animals, birds, and insects that had gone extinct in the last ten years. She had known that some species no longer existed, but as she'd read the avalanche of names, she had hardly been able to breathe. How could people let a whole species die?

Squirm swivelled in the front seat and faced her, his stubby, freckled finger pointing to a spot on a creased map.

"We're here," he said. "Just past Killarney. Won't be long now."

"Shall we stop and have a swim?" their father asked.

"No!" Robin wanted to swim, but she wanted to swim in her own lake. She gave Squirm a stern look, daring him to say anything different.

He got the message and faced the front. "We can go swimming when we get back."

Their dad pushed his fingers through his damp hair. "Must be a record breaker today."

"This whole summer is a record breaker," Robin said. It was kind of scary. After week after week of sizzling heat, lawns were yellowing, the leaves on the trees were shrivelling up, and small shrubs looked like bouquets of dry sticks. Would it ever rain again?

"Can I have a cookie, Dad?" Squirm reached for the tin he'd positioned beside him on the seat.

"Long as you give me one, too," their dad said.

Squirm handed him a cookie, gave one to Robin, and

took three for himself. He smirked at Robin. Payback for not arguing about the swim.

A raven cawed and Robin picked up her phone. It was a text from Zo-Zo.

New guy alert.

Robin texted back quickly. *Cool! Name?*

McCoy! Big B's stalking him already.

Brittany. *Figures,* Robin texted.

U can't have him either, Zo-Zo added. *U have Brodie.*

Brodie. Did she have Brodie? He'd been away at camp all summer and only written once. She wasn't sure she even liked him anymore. As a friend, yes, but as a boyfriend? Probably not. But it was too hot to think about that now.

Wanna swim when wr back?

Great! C u @ yr place!

She set the phone aside. Her eyelids felt as heavy as manhole covers. She let them fall to a close and gave herself over to the oblivion of sleep. When she woke up, the van had stopped. Were they home? Smelling gas, she opened her eyes. They were at a gas station in Parry Sound. Not far now. She pushed herself out of the van. The sun stung her skin as she yanked open the back door and pulled her bathing suit from her pack. She went into the washroom and slipped it on while her dad pumped gas. Now she'd be able to run down to the lake the minute they arrived home. Hotter than she'd ever felt in her life, she pushed her head out the window again. Her whole body felt swollen, bloated as if it were twice its normal size. And her skin was sticky as if she'd rolled in icing sugar. But soon she'd be in the lake, the cool lake.

The second she was back, she was going to jump in the water and stay there for days.

When they finally pulled up to the farmhouse, Zo-Zo was sitting in a deck chair on the porch. She waved frantically and leapt down the steps, the two dogs, Relentless and Einstein, charging behind her, their tails wagging.

"Welcome home!" Zo-Zo shouted.

The dogs jumped, spiralling in the air and yipping. Robin felt a surge of relief rise in her chest. She was home. *HOME.*

Zo-Zo threw her a towel and they ran down the path to the water.

When they got to the lake, Robin raced along the dock, then tried to stop herself. Zo-Zo and Squirm collided into her from behind. Relentless, however, did not stop. Nor did Einstein. They rollicked forward, flying off the end of the dock as if the water were clear and blue and beautiful.

But it wasn't clear and blue and beautiful. It was bright green and slimy and looked like something from outer space.

Wide-eyed, Robin stared out across the lake. The surface was covered in thick ooze for as far as she could see.

"Ew ..." Squirm cried, stepping back. "What happened to the lake?" His voice was barely above a whisper.

Shocked and horrified by what they saw, no one spoke.

CHAPTER TWO

Squirm plugged his nose. "Ew! It stinks!"

Robin waved her hand in front of her face. The lake smelled like a garbage bag that had been ripped open and left in the sun.

"Get the dogs out of the water," Griff shouted as she strode towards them. "It might be toxic!"

Robin made her voice sound commanding. "Relentless! Einstein! Come!"

The dogs continued to swim, seemingly oblivious to the yucky sludge the top of the water had become. Everyone yelled at them, frantic to get them out. After much shouting, the dogs made their way to the shore where they stood and shook, strings of green goo spinning off them.

Griff grabbed the dogs by their collars and pulled them towards the farmhouse. "I'll hose them down and put them in the barn to dry off."

A few moments later, Robin's dad came down to the dock.

"Dad, Dad!" Squirm called. "Something's happened to the lake! Look! What's the matter with it?"

Their dad walked to the end of the dock and made a visor of his hand, surveying the lake from one end to the other.

Robin followed his gaze. The lake, which was usually a shimmering mass of silver and blue, looked like a dense, green bog. It made her feel sick to look at it.

"What is it, Dad?"

"An algae bloom. A huge one."

"What's an algae bloom?" Zo-Zo asked.

"Just as it sounds," Robin's dad said. "It's algae — blooming! Algae are always growing, but sometimes, when it's been really warm, like this summer, they start to grow at an explosive rate." He leaned closer to the water. "There are different kinds of algae, but this one looks like a cyanobacteria —"

"Dad!" Robin didn't like it when he used terms she didn't understand.

"Commonly known as 'blue-green algae,'" he said. "When these bacteria die, they sink to the bottom and wipe out the oxygen other plants and fish need. It can be very toxic. We need to keep all the animals away from it."

"But the dogs …" Robin said, her voice cracking.

"They should be alright," her dad said. "Griff said they weren't in it long."

Robin tried to calm herself. Was Relentless going to be okay?

"I want our lake back," Squirm said.

"You and every other cottager," their dad said. "Maybe now they'll listen when we tell them not to use phosphates or clear the weeds from the shoreline."

Robin looked at her dad. "How do we make it go away?"

"I'm not sure we *can* make it go away," her father said. "It would have been a lot easier to prevent it."

Robin felt her frustration rise. "Isn't there *something* we can do?"

Griff came back on the dock and gave Robin a hug. "Not much of a homecoming for you two!" She looked worriedly at the lake. "It started yesterday. I didn't really know what to make of it."

Squirm picked up a twig, stuck it into the lake, and pulled it out. It looked as if it had been dipped into a can of bright green paint.

Their dad pushed his hands deep into the pockets of his shorts and made fists of them. "I'll call Don, the head of our Lake Association. We need a meeting."

Zo-Zo shook her head. "That's all adults ever do. Have meetings. And nothing ever changes."

Griff looked stern. "We'll have people's attention now." She turned to her son. "Time to talk to people again about using non-phosphate detergents."

Zo-Zo blinked. "As if changing detergent is going to save the planet."

"Every little bit helps," Robin's dad said.

Zo-Zo shrugged, looking unconvinced.

A few days later, Robin was making toast in the kitchen and listening to the radio. Her father had already left to help set up chairs at the community centre where an emergency Lake Association meeting was going to be held later that morning. She wondered whether the community centre was air-conditioned. She couldn't remember. A trickle of sweat ran down the small of her back. How could it be this hot so early?

A few feet away, Squirm was sitting at the kitchen table, swinging his head from one side to the other, humming as he drew pictures of bugs on some scrap paper. Beneath the chair, he was kicking his legs back and forth in a rhythmic way, as steady as windshield wipers.

Robin tried to butter her toast and bat away a mosquito at the same time and ended up getting butter on her arm. She was licking it off when she heard something on the radio.

"Sh!" She said to Squirm and turned up the volume. "Listen."

The voice on the radio was matter-of-fact. "The Health Unit recommends that people avoid all contact with lake water, including those activities that may result in inadvertent exposure, such as irrigating lawns and watering gardens. Symptoms of illness can include headaches, fever, diarrhea, abdominal pain, nausea, and vomiting."

"Yikes," Robin said.

Squirm looked up. "Dad was right. The water *is* toxic."

Robin tensed. "Where are the dogs?"

"Einstein's here at my feet," Squirm said. He strained his head up so he could see out the window. "Relentless is over there under the apple tree."

Robin sat down, relieved. She picked up her piece of toast, but the mosquito was hovering around it, so she set it down again and grabbed at the bug. Sure she had it, she opened her fist only to find it empty. Looking up, she saw it sailing through the air and swatted it again, but it simply careened away, flying through the air towards Squirm, its legs hanging like long stilts beneath its body.

"You'll never get it that way," Squirm said. "Watch this." He held out his arm and waited until the mosquito landed on his skin.

Robin sucked air in through her clenched teeth. How could he stand to let it land on him like that? "Smack it before it bites you."

"That's what you have to let it think — that it's about to get your blood. You even have to let it start to stick its stinger in. That's when it gets really excited, so excited that it doesn't notice your other hand coming down and —"

He moved the forefinger of his free hand over the mosquito and squashed the unsuspecting bug.

"Cool, eh? I call it the Squirm Squish. Works every time." His face split into a wide grin. "Can I have your toast?"

Robin nodded and watched as Squirm spread it with a thick layer of marmalade. Squirm didn't eat toast with marmalade on top, he ate marmalade with a thin layer of toast underneath. He wasn't interested in jam, only marmalade. Because it was orange. He loved anything orange — orange food, orange clothes, orange drinks. The orange juice jug in the fridge was usually drained down to the last few drops.

"I'm surprised you don't just spoon the marmalade right into your mouth," Griff said, coming in.

Squirm smirked. "Last time I did that, you yelled at me."

"I didn't yell."

Griff tousled his copper-coloured hair and turned to Robin. "Where's Gord?"

"Setting things up for the Lake Association meeting," Robin said.

Griff nodded. "Good. Is Zo-Zo coming? Do we need to pick her up?"

"Yup," Robin said. "She didn't want to come, but her dad is making her take photos for the paper. Besides, she wants to see if the new boy shows up."

Griff's thick grey eyebrows arched like birds' wings. "A new boy.... Must be the family that bought the old Simpson place. I think I saw him out front the other day. He's a real looker."

Robin smiled at the phrase.

"Laura told me her nieces are already fighting over him. Wouldn't want to see you and Zo-Zo get into a cat fight over a boy."

As if that could ever happen, Robin thought. She stood up and headed for the shower. Squirm grabbed her arm.

"Can we go swimming in another lake this afternoon — one that doesn't have an algae bloom?"

Robin didn't know what to say. It was a good idea, but it made her feel disloyal. Like going off to play when a friend was sick. She turned to Griff.

"How long until we can swim in our own lake again?"

The lines on Griff's forehead deepened. They looked like gashes.

"Don't think it'll be any day soon." Her large hands stroked her braid of white hair. "Swimming might just be over for the season. In our lake anyway."

Something hot and angry rose up in Robin's chest. How could this have happened? Maybe what Zo-Zo was telling her all summer was true — things in the environment had gone way too far.

She dragged herself upstairs and got into the shower, making it as cold as she could stand. The water came from the well, deep in the rocks, and she could always count on it to be cold. She let it pound against her, grateful for the goose bumps that began to pock up on her skin. When she started to shiver, she got out. By the time she put on her shorts and t-shirt, she was hot again.

"Let's go," Griff said the moment Robin came downstairs.

On the way to the van, Robin walked over to Relentless who was curled up under the apple tree beside the lane. Some apples had fallen and were lying on the ground around her. Usually, Relentless would be chomping them down as fast as they fell, but not today. Today she looked listless and her eyes were dull.

Worried, Robin pulled Griff over and they both kneeled beside the dog.

"She doesn't look very well, does she?" Griff said and pressed her lips together. "Probably took in some of the algae water."

Robin felt uneasy. "Will she be okay?" She knew the lake water was toxic, but could it kill a dog? What if it killed Relentless?

"Relentless is pretty healthy," Griff said. "Hopefully, she'll be able to slough off whatever was in that water. She'll come around."

Relentless looked at Robin with mournful eyes and Robin rubbed her ears. "Should I put her inside?"

Griff shook her head. "Leave her outside where she can feel the earth and smell the breeze. Let Mother Nature take care of her."

Reluctantly, Robin got up and followed Griff to the van. Squirm climbed in too and they dropped him off at his friend's place where he was working on an insect project for school, then they picked up Zo-Zo.

Zo-Zo stuffed her big, green knapsack between her feet and pulled out a large, yellow, spiral notebook. "I was researching all the things that can go wrong with lakes last night. Turns out, they can get sick just like people do. They can even die! In fact, a bunch of them already have."

Robin swallowed. She didn't want to hear any more. She wished she were sitting by the door so she could put her head out into the wind. Even though all the windows were open, she was sandwiched between two warm bodies and the air conditioning still wasn't working. It was too much. Maybe she should have stayed home and sat in the shade with Relentless.

Zo-Zo continued. "The Aral Sea, for example. It used to be one of the four biggest lakes in the world, but it's puny now. All but dead. Some scientist dude said it was one of the planet's worst environmental disasters."

Robin wasn't even sure where the Aral Sea was.

Zo-Zo let out a long, slow sigh. "Tons of lakes are sick like that. And when a lake gets sick, so do all the fish and stuff that live in it. I read somewhere that whales are really endangered. I love whales and —"

Griff's hands tightened on the steering wheel. "Our lake will recover. We'll make sure of that."

Zo-Zo raised her shoulders and dropped them again. "People said that about the Aral Sea. But it was too late."

Griff cast a concerned look at Zo-Zo. "You're sounding awfully pessimistic. Is everything okay? Is your mom alright?"

Robin had never met Zo-Zo's mom. She had left Zo-Zo's dad by the time Robin had moved here, and now lived in another city with some guy Zo-Zo called an "idiot." Robin knew Zo-Zo worried about her.

"I haven't talked to my mom in ages," Zo-Zo said. "She's not answering her phone. Or my emails."

"That's unsettling," Griff said. "Maybe I could drive you down to the city one day and we could go and visit."

Zo-Zo jerked her head towards Griff. "Would you? Would you do that?"

"Of course. She's your mother. You need to see her and know she's alright." Griff glanced at Robin. "Maybe all three of us could go. Make a day of it, what do you think, Robin?"

"Sure," Robin said. "We could check out those cool stores on Queen Street."

"Sounds like a plan." Griff pulled into the parking lot of the community centre. They all got out and Griff went in search of Robin's dad, while the girls joined the people crowding into the community centre.

Zo-Zo elbowed Robin hard. "That's him!"

"Who?"

"McCoy. The new guy!" Zo-Zo leaned in close. "Look at those shoulders."

Robin looked at the back of the boy who was walking a few yards ahead. Muscular and athletic looking, his arms were bronze coloured from the sun and his blond hair curled at his neck. Zo-Zo always went for this type of boy. Robin wasn't certain if she liked a "type" at all. Sure, it was nice if a boy was good-looking, but there had to be something else. She couldn't explain it, but it was different from what Zo-Zo liked. Which was good. For if the two of them ever liked the same boy, Robin knew that she was one who would be the loser. Zo-Zo was way better looking than she was.

Zo-Zo made sure they stayed close behind McCoy as they went into the building and when she saw which aisle he was heading towards, she hustled Robin into the row of seats behind. When he sat down, she grabbed the two seats directly to the back of his chair. Robin followed, always amazed with the way Zo-Zo went after what she wanted.

Zo-Zo drew a heart in the air just behind his back and suppressed a giggle.

As if sensing the emotional commotion behind him, McCoy turned in his chair. He saw Robin first and looked deep into her eyes. Robin tried to look away, but couldn't. Their eyes seemed fused somehow. His were big and brown and reminded her of her mother's.

She felt her breath stop. She didn't want her breath to stop. Nor did she want her chest to feel like it was full of butterflies. Her throat was dry and her face was hot. What was going on?

He was the most beautiful boy she'd ever seen. With clear skin, huge dimples and thick, golden hair and a face so angelic, so sweet and warm and playful that it made her smile even though she had no intention of smiling. His beauty was stunning.

Zo-Zo's voice broke the spell. "Hey, McCoy! Remember me? We met at the Dairy Queen the other night? You were with Big B — I mean, Brittany —" She fidgeted with a whale pendant she was wearing around her neck.

He turned his gaze to Zo-Zo and Robin felt the room dim as if the sun had just gone behind a cloud.

"Yeah, Zo-Zo. Hi." He looked at Robin and the sun came out again. "And who are you?"

"Robin. I'm Robin," she managed to say. Her voice sounded low and smoky. No wonder. She was on fire.

"She *has* a boyfriend," Zo-Zo said pointedly.

"No, I —" Robin jabbed Zo-Zo. Why couldn't Zo-Zo mind her own business?

"Most of the good ones do," McCoy said, shrugging his large shoulders ever so slightly as if this were only the smallest concern. His entire face lit up with a smile. Robin could feel her skin tingling from the force of it.

Up front, someone tested a microphone and then an official sounding voice called the meeting to order. Robin knew she should pull her eyes away from McCoy and give her attention to the meeting, but she couldn't. She was like a deer frozen in a car's headlights.

McCoy didn't seem in any hurry to look away either. "Hey, you're the one who runs that animal place —"

"We run it together," Zo-Zo said. "It's called 'The Wild Place.'"

"Can I come and see it?"

Robin tensed. As a rule, they discouraged visitors to The Wild Place. The animals needed to rest and recuperate. They didn't need people staring into their cages and poking their fingers through the wire.

"Sure," Zo-Zo said and pulled out her notebook. In her big, bold writing, she printed the phone number of the shelter. "And here's my email," she said and gave him the paper. "Just let us know when you want to come."

McCoy took the paper, mouthed the word "later" and turned in his seat.

The room quietened and Griff slipped into the seat on the other side of Robin. She glanced at Robin, glanced away, then looked back again. "You okay? You look like you've been hit with a two-by-four."

Robin swallowed, but said nothing. That was exactly how she felt.

The meeting began and various people stood up and talked about the algae bloom and debated what they thought the Lake Association should do about it. A representative from the Health Department talked about how important it was to not touch the water or use it in any way. "Not even for washing vegetables," she cautioned.

"But the lake is the only source of water we have," one of the cottagers complained.

Zo-Zo crossed her arms as the meeting droned on. She leaned towards Robin. "Blah, blah, blah." Robin suppressed a yawn. The meeting was going on forever. And as yet no one had even been able to suggest what to do other than wait for the algae bloom to fade away when the cooler weather arrived. The lake was sick, very sick, yet no one had any idea how to help it.

It was weird. She knew the lake was a living thing, but still, she'd never thought of it needing care. She'd just imagined that it would go on and on. But nothing went on and on. Her mother's death had seared that point into her like a hot iron into flesh. You had to take care of things. You had to not take them for granted. Because one day, they might not be there.

Various people stood up and talked, but Robin found herself staring at McCoy. His hair looked silky and she imagined what it would feel like to touch. She thought she could smell a slight whiff of ripening apples arising from it, but she couldn't tell. She caught herself leaning towards him and pulled herself back.

Beside her, Zo-Zo kept shifting in her seat. Finally, she said, "I better get some photos or my dad will kill me. Be back in a bit."

Robin watched Zo-Zo creep up close to the stage and take various shots. Then she slipped out the side door.

Robin wished she could go outside for a few minutes too. This meeting was going nowhere. Now people were debating whether global warming was actually real. Wasn't the condition of the lake proof of that?

Then the meeting was over. Griff stretched and went off to talk to Robin's dad. McCoy slipped into the empty chair beside her.

"So, when can I come and see The Wild Place?"

"Anytime," Robin said. If Zo-Zo was going to make an exception for McCoy, then she could too. She tried to think of a day that would be good, but was finding it hard to think with the fullness of his attention on her.

"Maybe Tuesday. Zo-Zo always comes in on Tuesdays and —"

"Zo-Zo doesn't have to be there …"

Robin felt scrambled and confused. What was he saying?

"I know Zoey is your friend and everything, but all she ever talks about is the environment. It's boring."

His words stung. Zo-Zo boring? Zo-Zo was the most interesting person she knew. So unlike the other girls at school whose only concerns were the state of their hair and fingernails.

McCoy flashed her a smile. "Don't get me wrong, I think it's cool the way she cares about the environment and everything, but don't you ever wish she'd talk about something else?"

Guiltily, Robin nodded. It was true. Sometimes Zo-Zo could be a little obsessed with the state of the planet. Especially lately.

"I could come tomorrow? Will you be around then?"

Robin tried to think. Hadn't Zo-Zo said something about an event tomorrow? Robin tried to remember. It was important to remember. If she scheduled McCoy for a day Zo-Zo couldn't be there, Zo-Zo would be upset with her. She tried to move her mind through the various things Zo-Zo had said about her schedule, but her mind felt airy and as hard to direct as a balloon.

She pulled her eyes away to ease the intensity of his gaze and looked down. McCoy was wearing new running shoes. They had neon green stripes on the sides and looked like the kind that cost a lot of money. She was wearing running shoes too, but hers were old and spotted with pine needles and mud. She felt embarrassed by them.

"I could come in the morning," he prompted.

"Sure," she heard herself say.

McCoy's face lit up. "Great! See you then." He stood,

waved at an older man who looked like his father and followed him out of the community centre.

"Darn. I missed him," Zo-Zo said, arriving just as McCoy went out of the building. She stared after him, her eyes wistful. "I want that boy."

A small grenade exploded in Robin's mind. Zo-Zo was going to a picnic tomorrow with her aunt and uncle. She'd mentioned it a few times. How could Robin have forgotten? And now, to make matters worse, she'd told McCoy he could come tomorrow — the very day Zo-Zo wouldn't be there. Zo-Zo was going to be furious with her.

Her mind raced. What was she going to do? Run out to the parking lot and hope McCoy and his dad hadn't driven off? She'd feel stupid doing that. But if she didn't, she had no way of getting in touch with him.

Zo-Zo was scrutinizing her face. "What were you two talking about?"

Flustered, a word slipped out her mouth. It was the same word she used when she didn't want to answer Griff's questions.

"Nothing."

Zo-Zo stared at her as if trying to figure something out.

Robin turned away. But she couldn't turn away from the shame she felt inside. She'd never lied to Zo-Zo before. Never.

CHAPTER
THREE

The crazy thing about lying was the way one lie created another. It was as if a single lie couldn't stand to be by itself and wanted to have another to keep it company, because the moment Robin lied about McCoy asking to come over, she realized she was going to need another lie to explain how his visit had come to be arranged in the first place.

Robin lay in bed partially covered by a thin sheet. The sheet felt as hot and thick as a wool blanket. Her bare feet were sticking out the bottom, but she was sweaty. Even Relentless had crawled out from her usual burrow under the covers and was now lying on the floor by the bed.

Robin tried to get herself to figure out what she was going to say to Zo-Zo, but the heat seemed to be cooking her brain, making her mind slow and sluggish. She reached over to the night table and snapped on the fan, then positioned herself so the cool air feathered against her face. Ah. Lovely. If only she could stay in front of the fan all day. When was this heat wave ever going to end?

In other summers, when a day or two got impossibly hot, she'd always had the option of cooling off in the lake. Sometimes she even started her day with a swim, but she couldn't do that now. And she missed it.

She checked the time. In a few hours, McCoy would be here. She sat up, excited, but worried. What if she didn't say anything to Zo-Zo about McCoy's visit at all? Would Zo-Zo find out? Probably. There would be too many other people who would see him here — Griff, Squirm, Laura, maybe even Ari — any of them might say something to Zo-Zo. No, it was too risky not to say anything. She was going to have to come up with something, but what?

If only she'd told Zo-Zo the truth right from the start. She wasn't sure why she hadn't. But how did you tell a friend that the boy she liked wasn't interested in her? No, it was worse than that. She would have had to tell Zo-Zo that not only wasn't McCoy interested in *HER*, but that he was coming on to someone else. And that someone else was Robin.

Robin wasn't used to boys coming on to her. Any boys, let alone one as gorgeous as McCoy. Why her? A boy as good-looking as he was could have his pick of girls. Zo-Zo had already mentioned something about Brittany stalking him. *Don't get your hopes up,* a voice inside her cautioned. *Give him the tour of The Wild Place, but don't be surprised that once school starts and the other girls see him, he'll forget you even exist.*

She frowned. At least then, if he still wasn't interested in Zo-Zo, it wouldn't be her fault. The last thing she wanted was Zo-Zo to be mad at her. So, even though it meant lying again, her only option was to tell Zo-Zo that McCoy had just shown up, out of the blue, and act as if she'd been surprised too.

But after that, she told herself: *No more lying!* She sighed. She didn't like lying. Lying made her feel unwashed somehow, as if she hadn't showered in weeks. And she would have sworn that lying had a smell to it too. Like body odour.

Robin dressed and wandered down towards the water. Or what used to be water. Now it looked like a radioactive swamp. Usually on Labour Day weekend, the lake was crowded with boaters and water skiers all getting in their last rides before school started, but today, the lake was eerily quiet. The same garbage-like aroma wafted from its surface.

It was hard to believe that something once so blue and beautiful could become so ugly so quickly. It was scary. Very scary. It made her feel helpless. Like she was standing beside a sick friend and unable to help in any way. But there was nothing she could do, nothing anyone could do. Even the Lake Association people, who were going to do tests and check people's septic systems, admitted that everyone was just going to have to wait for the cooler weather to inhibit the growth of algae.

It was depressing. So depressing that she turned away and walked to the barn. Laura, her dad's vet assistant, waved from across the yard, her round moon face beaming.

"You look nice," Laura said.

Robin blushed. She'd put on some decent clothes today rather than her grubby barn stuff, but she didn't think she looked dressed up. She didn't want to look dressed up.

"Something special happening today?"

"No."

She was lying again. Hadn't she just promised herself she was going to *stop* lying? Yes. So she added, "A kid from our Lake Association meeting is coming over to see The Wild Place. I figured it was okay. We don't have many animals in right now."

Laura nodded. As usual, she didn't make a fuss about things. That was probably why her dad liked her so much. Sometimes they even went out on dates. But that was as far as things had gone. And as far as Robin wanted them to go. She wasn't ready for her dad to have an official girlfriend yet.

"You talking about that new boy you were sitting beside at the meeting?" Griff asked, appearing from the barn. "The one you and Zo-Zo were drooling over?"

"We were *NOT* drooling!" She hated it when Griff kidded her.

Griff smiled at Laura. "The boy's face would make an angel sing."

"Sounds like trouble," Laura said.

Griff snorted. "Yeah, they're the ones that break your heart in half like a dinner plate."

"There was a boy like that at my high school," Laura said. "We called him 'Heart Break Hotel.' I cried an ocean over that boy." She shook her head. "Someone told me he's on his third marriage now. Good looks don't guarantee happiness." She pressed her teeth down on her bottom lip and gave Robin an anguished look. "Be careful."

Griff waved her huge hand through the air. Robin could feel the breeze from the motion.

"Getting your heart bashed up a bit is part of growing up," Griff said. "You and Zo-Zo can sop up each other's tears." She glanced around the yard. "Where is Zo-Zo anyway?"

Robin swallowed. "At a picnic. She'll be here later."

"Zo-Zo's letting you have this boy all to yourself? That doesn't sound like Zo-Zo!"

Robin swallowed. "She doesn't know."

A warning glance passed between Griff and Laura. Griff nodded slowly. "The plot thickens."

"I didn't know how to tell her," Robin said. There, at least she'd fessed up to part of it.

Laura checked her watch. "As much as I hate the idea of missing 'Angel Face' and a possible cat fight, I've got to go. I'm selling my strawberry jam at the market. With the lake out of commission, town will be packed. I'd better hustle."

She waved and went off. Robin waited for Griff to say more. Griff opened her mouth to speak, but the phone rang and Griff went off to answer it.

"Saved by the bell," Robin whispered and went into the barn. She wandered all the way to the back where the beaver lived. Although their policy was always to try and return animals and birds to their natural environment, it wasn't always possible. This beaver, for example, had had his tail severed by dynamite, the same dynamite someone had used to blow up his den. Miraculously, he had lived, but he'd never be able to survive again in the wild, so they'd given him a small pond to live in and brought him branches every day.

Robin loved watching him and she was grateful that he let her. He always hid when Griff or her dad came near, yet somehow the beaver trusted her. She sat near him and watched as he chewed the bark off one of the branches piled in the corner of his enclosure. He would go through the whole pile before the day was out. His teeth were slightly orange in colour and very sharp — sharp enough to chew through a tree as wide as her hand. How they knew which trees to eat was beyond her, but a single beaver could change a field into a swamp in no time.

Griff called swamps "mother nature's nurseries" because of all the new life they spawned. Robin didn't know much about that, but she knew she liked beavers.

Hearing Relentless bark outside the barn, Robin spun around to see McCoy coming towards her. Relentless was wagging her tail at his heels.

"Whoa! Cool! Is that a beaver?"

Robin nodded and watched as the beaver disappeared into his pond. Self-conscious, she bent down and petted Relentless. Her dog was acting like her old self again. Was this because of McCoy?

McCoy frowned as the beaver hid itself away. "I've never seen a real beaver before."

"If we're quiet, he might come back. Beavers don't have the best eyesight." She put Relentless out of the barn and came back to McCoy. He was standing very still, his camera at the ready. As she moved closer to him, she felt warm and bright, as if she were stepping into sunshine.

Soon, the beaver came out again and McCoy took pictures. He leaned close to Robin and whispered. "I want you in the photos too."

He stood back and held up his camera. "Adventure Girl saves another animal." He grinned.

Robin felt uncomfortable. He made it sound like she was some sort of hero.

"Actually, it was Griff who brought him in...." Robin steered him towards some other cages, but McCoy's eyes stayed riveted on her.

"You are kind of famous."

"I — I —" Hearing herself start to stammer, she used more force to get the words out. "I don't think so."

"Not every kid stands up to the sheriff and chains herself to a barn."

Robin tried to explain. "We were waiting for our wild animal licence and the sheriff was threatening to take the animals and ..." She looked at him curiously. "How do you know all this anyway?"

"My dad just got a job in the sheriff's office. They still talk about you down there." His eyes radiated admiration. "They say you've got a real way with animals."

Robin didn't know what to say. People often said this to her, but she was never sure what to make of it.

"Come on," McCoy said. "Show me the rest of the place."

They wandered from one area to another, peeking in every enclosure. She wished there were some babies to show him — baby animals had a way of bursting a person's heart open, making them coo and croon — but McCoy was enthralled with the animals that were there — a turtle with a foot badly cut by a fishing lure, a raccoon that had been shot with an arrow, a hummingbird that had lost most of its feathers.

McCoy looked pained as he viewed the grey stubble on the hummingbird's body. "What happened to it?"

"She got caught in some of that sticky fly paper," Robin said.

"Yeow. That had to hurt."

Robin put out her finger and the hummingbird stepped on it, pinching her skin with its tiny feet.

"Will she perch on my finger too?"

Robin tried to pass the bird along to McCoy's outstretched finger, but it kept hopping back to hers.

"See? It only wants you."

They moved on to other enclosures and finally to the surgery area where her dad did operations and other veterinary work. As they walked, she felt revved up somehow and slightly woozy. If she hadn't known better, she'd have thought she was coming down with the flu.

McCoy asked a lot of questions and she was glad. The questions helped her stay focussed. She avoided looking into his eyes. She knew if she did that, she'd start stuttering or say something stupid.

They were coming out of the surgery room when McCoy looked up into the rafters. "Oh, look, an owl."

Robin laughed, then stopped herself. She didn't want McCoy to think she was laughing at him.

"That's Owlie. He was my dad's pet when he was a boy. Griff wanted to keep him around, so she had him stuffed. Now he scares away the mice."

"Griff?"

"My grandmother. She works here too."

"Did I hear my name?"

They turned to see Griff coming towards them. "You must be McCoy."

Robin reddened. She didn't want McCoy to think she'd been talking about him.

"Great place you got here," he said.

"Glad you think so," Griff said and walked over to a pile of feed bags. She winced as she lifted one.

McCoy lunged forward. "Here, let me do that."

"Thanks," Griff said. "My back's been acting up lately —"

"I'll move them. Where do they go?"

Griff pointed to a corner of the barn. "See that cupboard over there? They need to go in there or the mice get into them —"

"No problem." McCoy took the bag from her as if it were made of Styrofoam. Bag by bag, he began stacking them where Griff had pointed.

Griff sat down on a hay bale near where Robin was standing. "A bit of brawn sure comes in handy sometimes." Together they watched him work.

"He seems nice enough," Griff said quietly. "Reminds me of a boy I fell for once."

Robin looked at her grandmother. Her face was pink and her eyes were full of merriment.

"What was his name?"

"Finn. Finn Rapier."

Robin could tell from the way Griff's mouth moved that she liked saying his name. Even now.

Griff patted her chest with her open palm. "I met him when I was already engaged to your grandfather. The timing couldn't have been worse. But goodness, he was so different, so daring and willing to be his own person. His very existence thrilled me."

Robin repeated her words. *His very existence thrilled me.* That's how she felt about McCoy.

"Sometimes I wonder what my life with him would have been like if I'd called off my engagement and married Finn instead of Frank."

Robin tried to picture Griff with someone other than her grandfather, but couldn't. Not that she'd known her grandfather well. She'd only met him a few times when she was very little, but still.

"I loved both of them," Griff said. "But I had to choose."

Robin was intrigued. "Do you think you made the right choice?"

"Absolutely," Griff said quickly. "Finn didn't want kids and that was important to me. Some things you can compromise on, and other things you can't. A person can't go against their basic nature. Not and be happy."

Robin fell quiet. If her grandmother had chosen Finn, would she even exist? The thought made her brain hurt.

"That's why you have to be careful who you decide to be with. Love is sticky. It glues you to someone. That's good in a way, 'cause it gets you through the bad times, but it makes breaking up hard...." Her voice trailed off.

"What ever happened to Finn?"

Griff lifted her shoulders. "Last I heard he was saving whales somewhere in the Antarctic."

"Saving whales! Wow." Zo-Zo was really into whales lately.

"Good thing someone is helping them," Griff said. "Whales are in real trouble. So Zo-Zo is always telling us."

Robin nodded. She didn't want to think about that now.

"Maybe Zo-Zo has heard of him," Robin said. Then she had an idea. "You should try and track him down.

Maybe he's on Facebook —"

Griff made a dismissive, grunting sound. "Probably has false teeth and a potbelly by now." She jerked her head back and forth. "Better to let sleeping dogs lie."

The phone rang again and Griff left to answer it. Alone now, Robin watched McCoy work. He had taken off his shirt and his skin was glistening from exertion. Strong and muscular, he had a kind of commanding sense about him. As if he knew exactly what he wanted and didn't want.

She heard the barn door creak and turned as Ari sauntered in. Dressed in white jeans and a cotton top with little silver sequins in it, she didn't look like she belonged in a barn.

"Squirm said your new boyfriend was out here."

Robin stared at her sister's mascara. It made her eyelashes look thick and inky.

"He's not my *boyfriend*. His family just moved into the Simpson's place."

Ari scanned the barn until she saw McCoy. "Not bad." She pulled some lip gloss from her tight jeans pocket and applied it. "Good catch."

Robin grimaced, but she couldn't stop herself from feeling pleased.

"Let me know if he has an older brother," Ari whispered. She winked and left the barn.

Robin continued to watch him. When he had hefted the last bag into place, he turned and let his huge brown eyes sink into hers. "I'm in love."

Robin felt her insides scramble. The intensity of his eyes, the closeness of his body, the "love" word — it was overwhelming.

He grinned. "It's that hummingbird. I can't stop thinking about her. She's so cute —"

Griff strode back in, van keys in her hand. Her face had that tense, we-have-a-rescue look on it.

"Robin, McCoy is going to have to go. We've got a rescue and I'm going to need your help."

Robin grabbed her rescue kit. In it were her heavy, protective mitts, a knife, a rope, and an array of basic medical supplies. "What are we rescuing?"

"A wolf. Or wolf-dog, I don't know which. Apparently he's been chained up for a while, so he's probably half-crazy with hunger. I don't have to tell you how dangerous that is."

McCoy looked at Griff eagerly. "Can I help? I'm strong and you might need to lift him. I'm good at stuff like that."

Griff worked her mouth between her thumb and forefinger as she considered what to do. "If he's badly undernourished," she said, thinking aloud, "we might have to bring him in. He'd certainly be too heavy for me and Robin to carry. We could use a sled, but there'd still be the problem of getting him into the van. That's *IF* we're able to get near enough to get a leash around him."

"Let me come and if I can help, great," McCoy said, grinning. "If not, I'll stay out of the way."

"As long as you *do* stay out of the way," Griff said. She nodded at him and the three of them hurried to The Wild Place van.

CHAPTER FOUR

As they drove to the rescue, Griff filled them in on the details. It had been the neighbour who had called. He'd heard howling and after a few days of it, had gone to look around.

"Apparently, the owner of the property is nowhere around. So the neighbour said, anyway. But that doesn't mean he won't show up while we're in the middle of things. Although that doesn't sound likely."

"And it's a wolf?" McCoy asked. He sounded excited.

"The neighbour said it was, but I'm thinking it's probably a mix between a wolf and a dog or a wolf and a coyote. Or Husky. It can be hard to tell the difference. But it's illegal to own a wolf in Canada, so I doubt if it's pure wolf. Be easier if it isn't."

"Why?" McCoy asked.

Robin liked that he was asking questions. She felt as if her own mind was on tilt. Sitting so close to him like this made it hard to concentrate. She could feel the heat of his body, smell the slight musk of his skin. She had to remind herself to breathe.

"Wolves aren't the friendliest when it comes to human beings," Griff said. "They see us as the enemy. As they should. If it does turn out to be a wolf, we'll have to be very careful."

"As they should?" McCoy asked.

Griff made a kind of harrumphing noise. It was a sound she often made when she thought something was obvious.

"We've practically wiped out wolves. Killed them for no reason other than we're scared of them. In some countries, like England, you couldn't find one if your life depended on it. Yet they used to be common over there."

Worried that Griff was going to go on a rant, Robin interjected. "What did the caller actually say?" It was always a good idea to get as much information as possible on the way to a rescue.

"That the wolf was chained up and that there was no sign of the owner and that there hadn't been for over a week. That means the animal is going to be starving. Starving and desperate."

Robin repeated the words her father had said to her a hundred times, saying them for McCoy's benefit more that her own. "And a desperate animal is a dangerous animal."

"That's right, Robin," Griff said. "I don't want any heroics."

McCoy glanced at Robin, his eyebrows raised. As if to say, *Is she always this intense?*

Griff continued. "Wolves can be dangerous at the best of times. That Big Bad Wolf thing in fairy tales didn't come out of nowhere. A starving wolf can be *very* dangerous. So don't go doing anything before checking with me."

McCoy raised his hand in a mock salute. "Yes, ma'am." He laughed.

It was a high-pitched laugh and Robin could hear the nervousness in it. She was glad he was nervous. Hopefully, that would make him cautious. She needed him to be cautious if they were all going to be safe.

"We haven't had anyone mauled or killed by a wild animal yet," Griff said. "And I don't plan to start now."

Robin thought about mentioning some of the situations that had happened at other shelters. The worst incident had occurred a few years ago when a woman had entered a wolf compound and been attacked and killed. Should she tell McCoy about it? She didn't want to scare him. Besides, it wasn't just wolves that were dangerous. All animals were dangerous if they became desperate. People were probably the same.

It was quiet in the van now and Griff turned down another road. As the van lurched, McCoy's body came careening into the side of hers. A few minutes later, the van turned the other way, and Robin felt her body pressing against McCoy's. She felt awkward about the way the van was pushing them together, but there was nothing she could do about it. Besides, it felt kind of exhilarating.

As they sped along, Robin suddenly realized they were now on the very road Zo-Zo would be taking to the family picnic. What if they drove right by each other? Zo-Zo would recognize The Wild Place van and be waving as she went by. What if Zo-Zo saw McCoy and her? Robin's stomach tightened.

"We're entering real hillbilly territory now," Griff said a few minutes later. "What I call 'the back woods.'"

Robin looked out at the fields around them. They were littered with abandoned cars and rusting farm vehicles and the few barns that still existed had faded to a dull grey and had missing boards. They reminded her of people with missing teeth.

"Not the kind of area that would be a bastion of animal rights," Griff said. "Real redneck country."

Robin was glad they had McCoy with them, just in case there was trouble. She checked the directions Griff had given her. "We must be getting close." Then she saw it. "There's the side road up there. Turn left."

They drove up the lane, passing a stained bathtub and other metal things Robin didn't recognise.

Robin read Griff's note out loud. "Says here to look for a house with a tire swing out front." She looked up and pointed. "I think that's the swing. Or *was* the swing." The tire had been cut in half and looked like two *C*'s moving in the wind. The house behind was badly tilted to one side.

"One whiff of wind and the whole place would topple over," Griff said. "We'll have to be careful. Very careful."

"Where's the wolf?" Robin said.

"Chained up somewhere," Griff said. "Which is good because it won't be able to run off. But it's bad, too, because when an animal is chained up, it can be aggressive. If it thinks we're going to hurt it, it's going to try and hurt us first."

"Maybe we can convince it we're friendly," McCoy said. "Is it a 'he' or a 'she'?"

"Don't know."

"Hopefully, it'll be a 'she.' I'm good with females."

"I bet you are," Griff said, her lips wobbling as she tried to suppress a smirk.

Robin gave her a stern look.

"Just remember," Griff said. "Wolves aren't like dogs. They're almost impossible to domesticate and usually, they don't want anything to do with humans." She reached into a bag and pulled out a handful of moose jerky. "But domesticated or not, this one's going to be hungry, so you better both take some food. Just check with me before you offer it. I don't want anyone losing any fingers. Got that McCoy?"

"Yes, ma'am."

Robin gave him a quizzical look. He sounded just like Squirm did when he had no intention of doing as he was asked.

"Let's check around the property first and leave the house till last," Griff said. "Peek in the windows if you want, but don't go in until you check with me. I want to make sure it's not going to fall down and kill somebody." She got out of the van. "Alright. Let's go."

They spread out and slowly started walking around the property. Robin checked out some sheds to the right of the house. They all had dirty windows, and as she peeked in, she could see that they were full of stuff — tires, old furniture, farm equipment — but there was no room for an animal in any of them.

When there were no other sheds to look at, she returned to the main house and went around to the back. She could hear McCoy speaking in a low voice. Was he inside? She crept forward until she was standing in the entrance of the house. The back door was ajar and she stepped into what looked like an old kitchen. The wallpaper was all ripped and curling and the wooden table and chairs has been tossed on their sides. As her eyes adjusted to the dim light, she could see McCoy crouched down. Why had he gone into the house when Griff had expressly asked him not to? She opened her mouth to say something, then saw the wolf.

A rope was tied around its neck and the other end was wrapped around a beam. At first she thought it was dead. All she could see was a skeleton of ribs and bones. Its fur was matted with mange and it looked severely emaciated. But its eyes were alive and fierce. And they were riveted on McCoy.

"It's okay," McCoy said. His voice was soft and melodic. "I won't hurt you."

"McCoy —"

It was Griff. Robin did not look at her. It was enough to hear the irritation in her grandmother's voice. Robin swallowed.

McCoy waved his hand in an attempt to get Griff to stay back. In a soft voice, he said, "She's trusting me, she —"

A piece of plaster fell from the ceiling. It landed with a *thunk* and sent a cloud of white dust billowing into the air. Robin tensed. Was the ceiling going to fall down on them? She saw the wolf's eyes widen in alarm, but it continued to stare at McCoy.

"Robin, stay by the door," Griff ordered. "But don't block it. One of us might need to get out of here — fast."

Robin edged back and McCoy started talking to the wolf again. She knew McCoy shouldn't have gone against what Griff had said, but she found it thrilling to watch the way he was with the wolf. He was so unafraid. And masterful.

For a moment she became lost in imagining herself and McCoy running The Wild Place, going out on rescues together, being a team, they —

"I'm going to cut the rope," Griff said. Keeping as far from the wolf as she could, she crawled around the side of the room. Watching the wolf the whole time, she sawed the rope with her pocket knife and held on to the end.

"Okay, McCoy. I think she's too weak to do any damage, so hold out some food for her. Let her smell it before you move your hand towards her. That's right. Now edge it forward."

McCoy moved his hand from side to side, letting the air carry the scent of the food to the wolf. The wolf's nostrils flared. McCoy inched the food forward until it was right in front of the wolf's muzzle.

Every muscle in Robin's body tensed. Was the wolf going to snatch the food out of McCoy's hand and take a finger or two with it?

The wolf's nose twitched slightly and she turned away.

"She won't eat it," McCoy hissed.

Robin sighed. She'd encountered this before. Sometimes an animal was just too far gone to take nourishment. It just didn't have the energy to live.

"Let me try," Robin said. She knew what to do.

"Okay, but be *careful!*" Griff said.

Slowly, very slowly, Robin inched her way out to the wolf. Speaking as soothingly as she could, she crawled forward until she was as near as McCoy. She took some jerky from McCoy and chewed it until it became a paste. Then she took it from her mouth with her fingers and reached her hand towards the wolf. It was hard to keep it from shaking. When the wolf showed no interest, even more slowly, she reached out and dabbed some of the wet paste on to the wolf's mouth.

The wolf tasted it with the tip of her tongue and then licked it more vigorously. Robin gave her more. The more the wolf ate, the more she seemed interested in eating and soon, she was eating the jerky right out of Robin's hand.

Robin put a handful of food on the ground right in front of the wolf and as she ate it, Robin slipped a leash around the wolf's neck. The next time she held food out to the wolf, she kept her hand several inches in front of the wolf and tugged gently on the leash. Wanting the food, the wolf stretched forward to get it.

"Good girl," Griff said. "Good girl."

Robin wasn't sure if Griff was praising the wolf or her, but she carried on, finally coaxing the wolf into standing. The moment she did stand and put weight on her left foot, her leg buckled and she sank down on her haunches.

Talking sweetly, Robin got her up again. This time the wolf kept her weight off the weak foot and managed to take a step forward. Robin rewarded her with food every time she moved.

It took a long time, but slowly, Robin got her out of the house and over to the van.

Griff arranged a plank of wood as a ramp and they continued to coach the wolf until she was inside. When she was, Griff tossed in several handfuls of moose jerky.

Robin watched as the wolf devoured the food. Now she knew where the expression "wolfing food down" came from.

With the wolf safely inside now, Griff closed the door of the van and leaned tiredly against it. She looked at McCoy with gentle but firm eyes.

"Disregard me again and you won't be welcome at The Wild Place."

McCoy opened his mouth to speak, but Griff held up her hand to stop him.

They all climbed in the van and Griff drove back slowly. No one spoke.

Robin didn't know what to say. Griff didn't make many rules, in fact, usually she let Robin and her siblings figure things out for themselves. But when it came to The Wild Place, she was a stickler about safety and insisted on certain protocols. If those protocols were ignored, she could be prickly as a porcupine.

Robin sighed. Too bad the day had turned so sour. If only she'd known, as they careened into The Wild Place lane, just how much worse things were going to get.

CHAPTER FIVE

The van rolled to a stop just in front of the barn. There, sitting on an old crate, was Zo-Zo, arms crossed, face glowering.

Robin felt every muscle in her body tighten. *Uh-oh.*

McCoy got out of the van and walked past Zo-Zo. "Hey," he said as he passed her and went to help Griff set up the ramp at the back of the van.

Zo-Zo's eyes went from McCoy to Robin, then back to McCoy again.

"What are you doing here?"

"Helping with a rescue," he said, as if he did one every day. He stretched out his arm and held out bits of moose jerky to the wolf while Griff picked up the rope and tried to ease the wolf out of the van. Slowly, it emerged and began limping down the ramp. When she was on the ground, Griff led her towards the barn.

Squirm appeared. "Whoa. Is she ever skinny."

Griff continued to coax the wolf along, speaking in soft tones as she went. She looked up at McCoy. "I can handle things from here."

Zo-Zo stared at the wolf with disbelieving eyes. "Is that a real wolf?"

"Yup," McCoy said.

Griff huffed. "Despite what our *expert* says here." She nodded towards McCoy. "I think she's got a bit of dog in her too." She looked up at Robin's dad, who was striding across the yard. "This animal isn't all wolf, is she, Gord?"

"No," he said. "Where did you pick her up?"

"Out by the lumber mill. She was tied up in an old farmhouse. There was no sign of the guy who lived there."

Robin watched her father dig his fists into his waist. She could almost feel his boney knuckles digging into his boney hips.

"He just left it to starve?"

"Looks that way," Robin said.

"He's the one who should be left to starve," Zo-Zo said bitterly.

"Take her to the surgery," he said. "I want to examine her paw." He followed Griff into the barn.

"Good thing the guy wasn't there or I'd have flattened him," McCoy said.

Robin was glad he felt so strongly. The way people treated animals was infuriating sometimes. More than infuriating. But, as her dad and Griff were always drumming into her, rescue workers had to keep that fury in check.

She lowered her voice. "Don't let Griff hear you say that. Not if you want to do more rescues."

"I *do* want to do more rescues," McCoy said. "That was the coolest thing I've ever done." He grinned at

Robin and Robin grinned back. She loved the idea of McCoy helping out.

Feeling Zo-Zo's hot stare, Robin quickly changed the topic.

"How was the picnic? I didn't think you'd be back so early." Darn! She was making it sound like she'd been trying to get away with something.

Zo-Zo's voice sounded as dead as a cat run over by a transport truck.

"My aunt wasn't feeling well. We came back early." She kept her eyes on McCoy as if trying to figure out something. "And what, you just, like, showed up?"

"I asked Robin if I could come and look around when we were at the meeting yesterday," he said in an easy tone. "She said 'yes.' So, here I am. Then the call came in about the wolf and —"

Zo-Zo's head snapped back as if she'd been hit. She closed her eyes, then opened them again and stared at Robin, her face contorting with emotion.

"You knew yesterday that he was coming today?"

Robin felt her body freeze. Her legs, her torso, her chest and jaw, all became rigid. Rock hard. Like a block of ice.

Zo-Zo stood up. "I've got to go."

"No reason to rush off...." McCoy said.

Somehow Robin got her hand to move and she reached out to stop Zo-Zo from leaving.

Zo-Zo yanked her arm away as if being touched by a poisonous snake. Stiffly, she strode down the lane to the road.

McCoy came and stood beside Robin. Together they watched as Zo-Zo became smaller and smaller until she finally disappeared in the distance.

"What's she so pissed off about?"

Robin opened her mouth to speak, but closed it again. How could she possibly explain it?

"She's just jealous," McCoy said.

Robin gave McCoy a sharp look. Did he know?

"She's the one who usually does rescues, right? So I guess she's mad that I got to do one."

Robin didn't say anything. It was too complicated. Besides, she knew if she said more, she'd start crying and she didn't want to cry. After all, it was her fault. If she hadn't lied, none of this would have happened.

McCoy's voice softened. "She'll cool down."

He lifted his arm and put it around Robin's shoulders. The warm power of him flooded through her. It startled her how strong the feeling was. It was as if her whole body was filling with a warm, radiant light. She could feel all her angst disappearing and an easy, golden feeling began to pervade her body. The peacefulness of it felt wonderful. Beyond wonderful. It had been so long since she'd felt like this. The last time had been before her mother died.

CHAPTER SIX

"Where's Zo-Zo?"

All weekend long, Robin had been asked the same question. *Where's Zo-Zo?* Squirm had asked it, her dad had asked it, and this was probably the third time Griff had asked.

Robin stared out the kitchen window. A light rain was drizzling down and the air was grey, so grey it looked as if the clouds had fallen to the ground and couldn't get up. There wasn't even a whisper of a breeze. She sighed. Now instead of just being hot, it was hot and sticky. It was *so* depressing.

"I don't know," she said. Zo-Zo had not shown up at The Wild Place all weekend. Now it was the holiday Monday and there still was no sign of her. Robin doubted whether McCoy would show up again today either, so it was going to be a long, lonely day.

"I guess she's mad about being left out of McCoy's visit," Griff said. "But you know Zo-Zo — she flares up like a firecracker, but she usually settles down quickly enough. Hopefully, once you both get to school tomorrow, this will blow over. And take this heat wave along with it."

Robin hoped so, but she wasn't sure. She had lied to Zo-Zo. *Lied!* Right to her face. No wonder Zo-Zo didn't want anything to do with her. What a bad friend she'd been. What if Zo-Zo never talked to her again? Feeling her stomach tighten, she pushed her cereal bowl away.

"You look like someone's peed on your cornflakes," Griff said. "Why don't you go and have a shower?"

"I did already."

"Then go to the barn and do something useful. That will get your mind off things."

Robin yanked on a rain jacket and went out, letting the screen door bang behind her. She liked the sound of it so much she was tempted to go back and bang it again.

Relentless loped along beside her, nose twitching as she scanned and assessed the smells in the air. At least Relentless was better now. Thank goodness for that.

When they got to the barn, Robin wandered to the back to see the hummingbird. It cocked its tiny head as she approached.

"Yes, I know it's time for breakfast. Are you hungry?"

The bird was flitting about in its cage. It was so tiny, not much bigger than her thumb. The skin on one side of its body still looked raw from where its feathers had been torn away. She couldn't imagine how much that would hurt. Like a person having all their hair yanked out.

"Don't worry," she whispered. "You'll fly again. I promise."

She made up some formula and watched as the hummingbird stuck its long, toothpick-thin beak into the formula and sucked it up. One day that same beak would be dipping into the throats of flowers once again.

Although it was hard to see the awful state some of the birds and animals were in when they came to The Wild Place, the good part was watching them get better. That was what made all the work worthwhile, knowing that their pain was temporary and that one day they'd be back in the wild.

Would her friendship with Zo-Zo recover too? They'd had spats before, but never a big fight like this. This one felt huge and very serious. Would they be able to get over it? Zo-Zo had looked disgusted when she'd left the other day. *Disgusted!* Robin had never seen Zo-Zo that upset before. At least not with her.

All weekend, Robin replayed what had happened. Over and over. At times she tried to put some of the blame on Zo-Zo, but it wouldn't stick. She herself had been the one to mess up everything. That fact made her feel all the more miserable.

Hearing someone come in, Robin turned. McCoy! It was McCoy! She could hardly believe her eyes. She hadn't expected him to come again today, but here he was. Her body suddenly felt as if she were a big helium balloon filling with air.

McCoy's face broke into a dimpled smile as he waved and pointed to the area of the barn where the wolf was. Robin nodded. He'd feed the wolf and then come and talk with her for a while. At least that's what he'd done yesterday.

She carried on feeding the hummingbird, but she felt optimistic now, lifted up somehow, as if she was in a hot air balloon and floating up and up, leaving all her irritations and problems behind.

"Told you being out here would cheer you up," Griff said, coming into the barn. She cocked her head and heard McCoy talking to the wolf. Leaning close to Robin, she whispered. "Oh, I get it. The object of your affections is here." She studied Robin's face. "You've got a hefty crush on this boy, don't you?"

Robin's face stung with heat. Did she? She'd had crushes on other boys, Brodie for example, but this felt different. She'd *liked* Brodie, in fact she still liked Brodie, but she never felt like she was being spun around in a blender the way she did with McCoy.

Griff pulled her mouth to one side so that it bunched up her cheek. "If only Zo-Zo didn't like him too."

Robin could feel the warmth of Griff's breath on her ear. She nodded solemnly.

Griff rubbed her jaw with her large hand. "Zo-Zo's an important friend. You don't want to lose her. Have you apologized for lying to her?"

Robin shook her head. "But I will," she whispered. "I'll apologize tomorrow when I see her at school." She didn't want this conversation with Griff right now. In fact, she wished Griff would just go away. So she could have McCoy to herself. Griff squeezed Robin's arm and went off.

Robin walked back to where McCoy was.

He grinned when he saw her. "There she is," he called. "Wild Animal Girl."

Robin felt her face break into a gigantic grin.

60

The next day, Robin arrived at school early. She wanted to make sure she got a chance to talk to Zo-Zo before class started. Once she found her new classroom, she put her things on the same seat she'd had last year and piled some books on the seat in front for Zo-Zo. It was the set up they'd had last year: Zo-Zo in front, Robin behind. That way, they could whisper to each other and exchange notes all day long. That was what Robin wanted, to have things go back the way they were before. She watched the classroom door, feeling nervous. And vulnerable somehow. For ages, Zo-Zo had been her best friend. Now it all felt weird.

Robin was getting her own books organized when McCoy come into the class, swarmed by a group of girls. It was just as Robin had imagined. All the girls were after him. When he saw her, his face brightened and he came towards her and put his books on the seat she was saving for Zo-Zo. The other girls reacted with surprise, looking at Robin with admiration and envy.

"I was saving that seat ..." she said. Even to herself, her voice sounded weak.

"Yeah, for me!" McCoy said, blasting her an irresistible smile.

"Lucky you," one of the girls said to Robin.

Robin was about to explain when Zo-Zo appeared in the doorway. Seeing McCoy at the desk she usually occupied, she stiffened and walked to the other side of the room. She took a seat in the last aisle, as far away from Robin as she could get.

Robin swallowed hard. Should she go after her? Try to explain? She was debating what to do when the teacher came in and class began. Robin sighed. Getting Zo-Zo back as a friend was going to be harder than she'd thought. She would try to talk to Zo-Zo at recess.

But when the mid-morning bell rang and everyone went outside, Robin couldn't see Zo-Zo anywhere. She was glad McCoy was standing beside her or she didn't know who she would have hung out with. A group of kids gathered around them, all wanting to meet McCoy. It was the same at lunch. Robin counted seven girls sitting at their table, all of them fawning over him.

These girls were all part of what Robin thought of as the "IN" crowd. They were the best looking kids, the ones that had the fashionable clothes and coolest parties. She'd always felt too different from them to even think about being in their group. But now, here she was, eating at their table, laughing at their jokes. She looked around for Zo-Zo, but again, couldn't see her.

As they ate their sandwiches, McCoy told the girls at the table about the wolf rescue. Robin could tell that he liked having an audience.

"You were *so* brave," Brittany said to McCoy, her eyes wide and adoring.

"Robin's the brave one. She *started* The Wild Place," McCoy told them. "All by herself."

"Zo-Zo helped," Robin said, but no one was listening.

"Weren't you worried the wolf was going to bite you?" a girl named Sienna asked.

Brittany held out her hand and appraised her bright red fingernails. "I'd be scared of losing my fingers."

The bell rang and on the way back to class, some of

the kids asked Robin questions about The Wild Place. It was strange. These kids had never shown any interest in the shelter before. Now, however, because of McCoy, they wanted to know all about it.

Even on the bus on the way home, she and McCoy were pestered with questions. Most were about him. Where had he moved from? Who was his favourite band? What did he like to do on weekends?

As McCoy talked, Robin looked for Zo-Zo. Usually, Zo-Zo took the same bus, but Robin couldn't see her anywhere. Was she walking home? Was she that determined to avoid her and McCoy?

"Can we come and see your wolf?" Caitlyn asked.

Robin winced at the word "your." The way everyone was talking it was as if The Wild Place and all the animals there belonged to McCoy.

"Sure!" McCoy said in a loud, commanding voice.

Robin felt something spike up along the length of her spine. If she'd been a dog, the hairs on her back would have been standing straight up. *Wait a minute. The Wild Place isn't a petting zoo.*

Robin leaned close to him and whispered, "The Wild Place doesn't allow visitors."

Caitlyn overheard and looked at Robin as if she'd just knocked a cookie out of her hand.

"You let *me* visit," McCoy shot back.

Robin felt stupid. "We make exceptions sometimes. But we don't want the animals getting used to people." Her stomach felt as if it had worms in it. Thousands of them, all squirming around. McCoy sounded so irritated. She tried to explain.

"If an animal gets used to one human, it will think *all* humans are safe. It might go up to someone once we've released it. That could get it shot." She considered saying what her father always said, "Wild animals need to be wild," but decided against it.

McCoy looked out the window. The bus slowed. It was Robin's stop.

McCoy jumped off the bus first and led the way towards the barn. The dogs ran up to them and fell in line behind McCoy like eager foot soldiers.

Robin sighed, but followed too.

CHAPTER
SEVEN

Robin tore some lettuce into little pieces and added a cut-up carrot. She yawned. She was tired and wanted to go to bed, but she needed to make her lunch for tomorrow. Should she toss in some tuna fish? No, tuna had a strong, fishy smell and she didn't want all the other kids at the lunch table to plug their noses when she opened her lunch bag. Besides, she'd been trying to be vegetarian for a while now.

After the whole fiasco with the factory-farm chickens, both she and Zo-Zo had tried becoming vegetarian, but Robin had found it very difficult. Especially when everyone else in the family ate meat and fish, everyone but Ari, who wouldn't eat red meat. McCoy ate meat too. It had been three weeks since the start of school and every day at lunch he pulled out a sandwich stuffed with turkey, chicken, bologna, or roast beef. He called what Robin ate "rabbit food" and kept offering her bites of his food, which she usually took. His sandwiches always tasted so good. She didn't want to like them so much, but she did.

Beside her, Griff was making Squirm a roast beef sandwich and the smell of it made her mouth water. That's a *cow*, she told herself. *A cow!* Her mouth stopped watering. When she thought of it that way, it wasn't so hard to resist.

She wanted to resist. Last year, she'd had the whole family do a carbon footprint test and it had surprised her how high their carbon use had been. The test had said that their high score was mostly due to eating meat. As she soon learned, meat eating involved lots of transportation and that was the problem. The web site went as far as to say that if everyone became vegetarian, the world's pollution would be cut in half. That fact astounded Robin and made her all the more determined to cut back. But it was hard.

Robin found the whole meat eating thing confusing. How could people say they cared about animals and eat meat? Griff, for example, adored animals, but like Robin's dad and everyone else in the family, she didn't think twice about eating a hamburger, or bacon, or chicken wings. Robin ate that stuff sometimes too. She wished she didn't, but she did. But she felt guilty about it. To lighten her guilt, she did lots of other things, like recycling. Which was more than a lot of the kids at school did. How could they say they loved nature, loved the birds and wildlife, then do all kinds of things to endanger it? How could people say they cared and then not care?

Robin spooned a dollop of homemade salad dressing on the greens. Now her salad smelled like a dill pickle. Why did Griff have to put dill in everything? Just because there were bunches of it growing in the herb garden didn't mean it had to be put in *everything*, did it? She grimaced and put the salad into a little plastic container and shoved it into her lunch bag. Hopefully, none of her new friends at the lunch table would say anything. They always seemed so ready to ridicule anyone or anything that was different. As if different was dangerous.

Robin looked out the kitchen window at the darkening sky. The night was coming so early now. In the waning light she could see some trees across the field that had already turned yellow and red. She didn't like the fall. Her mother had been sick in the fall and sad memories seemed to unhook themselves from the branches of her memory at this time of year and collect around her.

It didn't help that The Wild Place was all but closed now. She was already starting to feel cooped up. If only she could hibernate like a bear — crawl into a log, close her eyes and wake up in the tender light of spring.

But now that McCoy was in her life, maybe things would be different. Ever since the wolf rescue, he'd been coming to The Wild Place every day. Maybe one of these times she would get up her nerve and ask him to do something. Go for a bike ride or walk down to the creek. Once the snow came, maybe the two of them could go snowshoeing. Or build a bonfire out on the lake. She could feel the heat of the fire on her face now. McCoy's eyes were shining in the firelight.

"That all you're having? A salad?" Griff asked.

The picture of the bonfire dissolved and Robin was back in the kitchen again.

"Goodness, that's not enough to keep a bird alive. Why don't you toss in some nuts or something? For protein."

Robin thought about that. Nuts were fattening. Griff looked at her with concern. "You're not trying to lose weight, are you?"

Robin shook her head. She knew McCoy liked girls on the thinner side, but she wasn't going to say that to Griff.

Griff looked at her sternly. "Didn't you learn anything from what Ari went through?" She put her hands on Robin's shoulders. "You're fine the way you are. Don't go thinking you have to be thin to have a boy like you. That's just nonsense."

"I know that," Robin snapped. Just because Ari had gotten an eating problem for a while didn't mean she would have a problem too. Why couldn't Griff trust that she knew what she was doing?

Griff took a small bag of almonds from the shelf and tossed it to Robin.

"Just in case you get hungry."

Robin tossed it back. "They don't allow nuts at school anymore."

Griff sighed and put them away. Then she leaned against the counter. "How's it going with you and Zo-Zo? Are you two talking yet?"

Robin grimaced. "I wish you'd stop asking me that."

"I miss her," Griff said. "Don't you?"

Robin wasn't sure. For weeks now, Zo-Zo had been ignoring her and it hurt. Thank goodness McCoy still came to the shelter. Robin loved that. If Zo-Zo started coming around again, she would no longer have McCoy all to herself. And she liked having him all to herself.

"Good thing we've got McCoy helping," Robin said. "Did you see what he did with the new enclosure?"

Because of the wolf's leg injury, she couldn't be released to the wild, so they were fencing off a large area which would be her permanent home. None of them were happy about having to contain her, but at least the wolf wouldn't have to be put down or go to a zoo.

Griff nodded. "Has he given the wolf a name yet?"

Since McCoy was doing so much of the work involved with taking care of the wolf, they were letting him name her.

"Rebel. He's calling her Rebel."

Griff shook her head. "Sounds like a nickname McCoy should have for himself."

"McCoy is going to train her."

"He can try," Griff said, "but, as I've said, wolves aren't just wild dogs. You can't train them to give you a paw or any other such nonsense. Frankly, I don't know why anyone would want to. They're wild and they should stay wild."

"I told that to McCoy, but he said it's not very wild to have a wolf caged in an enclosure either."

"Did he now."

Robin could practically hear Griff's teeth grinding.

"Amazing how quickly that boy is becoming an expert on wolves. But then he was an expert from Day One, wasn't he? Disregarding everything I said when we did the wolf rescue."

That's why Griff doesn't like him, Robin thought. *She'd never forgiven him for not following her orders.*

"He put himself and The Wild Place at risk that day," Griff said.

Robin stared at her. Did Griff really think that? She waited for Griff to say more, but Griff took a deep breath and slowly let the air out.

"Enough about McCoy. I want to talk about Zo-Zo. She's been a good friend to you. That's not something you want to toss away lightly."

"I'm not tossing it away lightly," Robin said. "She's the one who's refusing to talk. Not me."

"I'm going to call her. See if she still wants to go to the city. Maybe all three of us can go."

Robin rolled her eyes. If Zo-Zo wouldn't talk to her at school, she doubted if she'd be willing to go with her to the city. Sometimes Griff's relentless positivity drove her crazy.

Suddenly, Griff's face beamed with delight. "Remember that time we got those baby racoons? You and Zo-Zo got up every four hours to feed them. For days and days."

Robin smiled in spite of herself.

"And remember how the two of you raided that factory farm?"

Robin would never forget the noise the chickens had made when Zo-Zo pulled them from their cages and flung them outside. Robin had thought her ear drums would burst. It made her ears sting even now, just thinking about it.

"Then there was that time when the sheriff came —"

"Before we got our licence —"

"Yes," Griff said. "He was going to impound the animals —"

Robin nodded. She'd been terrified.

"Wasn't Zo-Zo the first one to ride her bike over and help?"

She was. Robin couldn't deny it. Zo-Zo had even chained herself to the barn just as Robin had done.

Griff's eyes were intense and penetrating.

"That's the history you two share. And there's more to come if you two can patch things up." She was thoughtful for a moment. "Can't you work on some project together at school? Do something to get things going again?"

Robin thought about that.

"Our teacher said something about giving us a project on global warming. Maybe I could ask Zo-Zo if she wants to be my partner."

"Perfect! You both know so much about the topic."

It was true. Between the two of them, they *did* know a lot. So much that they would probably find it frustrating trying to work with anyone else.

"Ask her," Griff encouraged. "I'll call her too. Maybe between the two of us, we can fix things up."

Robin doubted it, but she knew better than to argue with her grandmother.

The next day, when Mr. Hutchinson gave the class a few minutes to pick partners, Robin got up her nerve and walked over to Zo-Zo's desk. Her palms felt damp.

Before she could open her mouth, Zo-Zo spoke.

"I'm working with Lewis," she said, turning to the boy who sat behind her.

Lewis's eyes ping-ponged back and forth from one girl to the other.

Robin forced herself to speak. "So that's it? We can't even work together anymore? Or be friends?"

"Friends don't lie to each other," Zo-Zo said. "Or dump the other for someone else." She cast her eyes across the room. "Which is what it looks like McCoy is doing right now."

Robin followed Zo-Zo's gaze. Brittany was standing by McCoy's desk with a triumphant look on her face.

Robin felt her heart sink to her feet. Now, not only didn't she have Zo-Zo as a partner, she probably didn't have McCoy either. And Brittany did.

Robin slunk back to her seat, sorry she'd even tried to repair things. She wasn't going to try again.

CHAPTER
EIGHT

Robin plunged the long, bristly brush deep into the bottle and pumped it in and out. Then she rinsed out the warm, soapy water and put the bottle in the drainer to dry. They washed the baby bottles every year in the late fall so that when spring came and they had babies here, there, and everywhere, all screaming for food, they'd be prepared.

Wash, rinse, drain. Wash, rinse, drain. Although her hands were busy, her mind was on something else: McCoy. It was Saturday and he'd just been here for a few hours, so she was feeling great. She always felt great after she spent time with him, but the moment he left, worries began to scurry across her mind, like mice after the lights had been switched off.

At school, the other girls were still all over him, but so far, he hadn't shown any particular interest in any one of them. He talked to them all, sometimes even flirted and joked with them, and he obviously liked their attention, but he didn't seem to favour one over another. At least not yet. She was hugely relieved, although she knew that could change in a heartbeat.

"Well, I talked to her," Griff said.

She turned to Griff. "Talked to who?"

"Zo-Zo! Have you forgotten about her already? Now that McCoy's on the scene?"

Robin felt like she had been punched. She used to feel that Griff understood her. That Griff was on her side. Now she was beginning to wonder.

"No," she said sullenly.

Griff let out a long, laboured breath. "I think she's really worried about her mom. And that's on top of all the stuff going on between the two of you." Robin wiped a pool of water on the counter, then began to rub hard at a tea stain. It wouldn't go away.

"McCoy says she's jealous."

"Of course she's jealous. You would be too if he'd chosen her instead of you."

Robin turned away. She hated it when Griff jumped on her like this. She rubbed the tea stain again.

"I'm sure you'd feel the same way if Zo-Zo were spending every hour of every day with McCoy instead of you."

"I'm not spending every hour of every day with him."

"You're either with him or talking about him."

"I thought you liked him helping out."

"I do. What I don't like is the way you're acting. As if he's the only thing that matters."

Shut up, Robin wanted to say. She turned to the pile of remaining bottles. When Griff was on her case like this, she just wanted to get away.

"It's McCoy this and McCoy that. I'm tired of it. There's more in the world than McCoy."

Maybe, but nothing that feels as good.

Griff's face softened. "Look, let's do that trip to the city. Just the three of us. Book ourselves into a hotel down by the waterfront and go for the whole weekend. Like we did last year. Remember the fun we had?"

Robin did remember. They had walked for hours along Queen Street, checked out funky clothing stores, wandered into tattoo parlours, ate in ethnic restaurants — did all the things they couldn't do in a small town. It had been fun.

"She won't go," Robin said.

"I think I can persuade her," Griff said. "She really wants to see her mom. So, I'll take her to her mom. That will be the main purpose of the trip. But we can go a day early and do some other things first. I won't tell her you're coming until the last minute."

Robin felt uneasy. The plan sounded devious. It wasn't like Griff to be devious. Besides, what would McCoy get up to if she went away for a weekend? There were so many girls out there, girls who would pounce if Robin wasn't around to keep an eye on things.

"I just think the three of us need to spend some time together. Like the good old days."

Robin didn't say anything. She began thinking about the gloating look on Brittany's face when she announced that McCoy was her partner for the Global Warming project.

"Besides," Griff said, "I think it would be a good idea for you to have a McCoy-free weekend."

Robin frowned. Griff was making him sound like a bad habit she should break. That annoyed her. McCoy was the most wonderful thing that had happened to her in a long, long while. Nothing Griff said was going to change that.

Griff draped the tea towel over the rung near the sink. "Come on, let's wander down to the lake and see how it's doing."

Even though it was sunny out, the air was cool. Robin knew she should put a jacket on, but hated giving in to the colder weather, so she pulled her hands up into the sleeves of her sweatshirt and followed Griff. She hadn't been down to the lake for a while, but now she forced herself to look at it. The surface was black and ugly.

"It looks awful, doesn't it?" Griff said. "But it's a good thing, really. The algae is dying. The cold weather is killing it. Thank goodness. By next spring you won't even remember it."

No, Robin thought. *I'll always remember.* "What if it happens again next summer?"

Griff shook her head. "I want to say it won't, but with all this global warming, I don't think any of us know how things are going to play out. But hopefully everyone's learned that this lake needs care. We can't take nature for granted like we used to."

Griff sat down on a rock near the shore and neither of them spoke. Robin stared across the lake to the far shore. With all the leaves down now, she could see the contours of the land so much more clearly and the cottages looked exposed.

Finally, Griff said, "Did I ever tell you about your Aunt Lucy's boyfriend?"

Robin shook her head. Aunt Lucy was Griff's sister and Robin had only met her a few times.

"When I was young, like a million years ago," Griff said, "Lucy fell in love with a boy; I think his name was Thomas. She wanted to make him happy, so she started to talk the way he talked and act the way she thought he wanted her to act. She became a totally different person. Just to please him."

"What happened?"

"He dropped her. Dropped her like a candy wrapper."

"But why didn't he like her even more?"

"Because when someone isn't being themselves, they lose something. Some sort of spark goes out and they become kind of dull." She shook her head. "Besides, it's confusing to people. Like it would be if a dog started acting like a raccoon."

Robin tried to picture that, but couldn't. Around her on the grey and pink rock, ants were scurrying around, as if on important missions only they knew about.

"What happened to her in the end?"

Griff rolled an acorn in her fingers. "After he dropped her, she cried for a while, but she met someone else. Someone who liked her for the way she was. So I guess it was a good lesson in the long run." She looked up at the sky and squinted. "She figured things out for herself. Just like you will." Her eyes found Robin's. "I know I get in your face about things, but I do trust you, you know. You'll figure things out."

Robin felt relief, but her relief was soaked in sadness. Ever since her mom had died, Griff had always been the one who understood her. Why couldn't she understand about McCoy? Why didn't she believe McCoy was good for her? He made her feel great. As if nothing was wrong, as if nothing was missing, as if everything was going to be alright. How could Griff tell her that she shouldn't want that?

Suddenly, Griff raised her arm and pointed. "Look. Over there. Isn't there some water showing on top of the algae?"

Robin squinted in the direction Griff was pointing. Yes, there, on the surface a few hundred yards away, she could see water, blue and sparkling. Maybe her lake was coming back to itself after all.

CHAPTER
NINE

Over the next few weeks, Griff kept harping about the three of them going to the city, so reluctantly, Robin agreed to go. Maybe once Griff saw how closed off Zo-Zo was to Robin, she would realize the impossibility of reviving their friendship and stop trying to get them together.

The day of the trip, Robin awoke to rain pounding on the shingles. It sounded like someone was up there banging their fists against the roof and having a tantrum.

Relentless stayed buried under the bedcovers and Ari poked her long, elegant arms out of the sheets and stretched. She yawned and spoke at the same time.

"Isn't this the day you're supposed to go to the city?"

Robin peered out the rain-splattered window. There was so much water that little rivulets were running across the yard. "Maybe Griff will call it off." They wouldn't be able to wander around the city if it was raining like this — and wasn't that the whole point?

"You wish," Ari said. "You know Griff. Once she sets her mind on something ..."

Slowly Robin got out of bed and dressed. At least she didn't have to worry about being too hot. The sweltering heat had ended, but now instead there was endless rain and thunderstorms. The weather had become so unpredictable. Was this global warming? She knew it was.

"Robin. Breakfast," Griff called up the stairwell.

Ari's eyes met hers. They said, *told you so.*

Robin pushed her body forward. She felt as if she was pushing a snowball uphill. Reluctantly, Relentless followed.

When she'd said yes, the idea of going to the city hadn't seemed so bad. Now, however, it felt awful. She was going to miss a party. *A party!* Caitlyn had announced a few days ago that she was having an all-girls pyjama party this weekend and Robin had been invited — a sure sign of belonging to the IN crowd. But she'd had to say she couldn't go.

Brittany was going to be there, so there was a good side to not going, but still. The only thing she was truly grateful for was the fact that it was an all-girls party. At least she didn't have to worry about McCoy and Brittany both being at a party she couldn't go to. That would have been the worst. She went into the kitchen. Raincoats and umbrellas were piled at the door.

"We're not going to let a little rain stop us," Griff said.

Robin crossed her arms, slumped down on a chair and watched as Squirm picked the orange Froot Loops out of his bowl. He always ate those first.

There was a loud rumble of thunder and then a flash of lightning.

Great, Robin thought. Surely Griff wouldn't go out in a full-fledged thunderstorm. That was dangerous, wasn't it? Relentless pressed her head into Robin's thigh. She was never easy in thunderstorms.

Griff smiled brightly. "It won't last. The forecast is for sun by early afternoon."

"Forecasts can be wrong," Robin muttered.

"They can also be right." Griff said cheerfully, putting a plate of toast on the table.

Robin pushed it away. If only she could push away the trip to the city. "I'm not hungry."

Griff tossed a banana into a bag and pulled on her bright blue raincoat. "Okay, let's go."

Robin petted Relentless goodbye. She felt as if she were going away for a week. She opened an umbrella and followed her grandmother to the truck. The rain spit on the plastic of her coat. She wanted to spit back.

Griff steered the truck slowly down the lane. Runnels of water were making ruts in the mud. Griff clicked on the windshield wipers and they jutted back and forth. *Whack, whack, whack.* They cleared the glass for a moment, but the rain was heavy and blurred the view almost right away.

It was stupid to be driving in this weather. Stupid.

"There," Griff said. "It's easing up."

Robin frowned. *No, it isn't.*

Griff drove through the downpour, ploughing through the puddles with enough speed that huge wings of water splashed up on either side of the truck.

Robin knew Griff was trying to make her laugh, but it wasn't going to work. Not today. Resentment skewered her into the corner of the truck. Griff could make her go, but she couldn't make her enjoy it.

A few minutes later, they pulled up in front of Zo-Zo's house and Robin felt her spine stiffen. What if Zo-Zo refused to talk to her? That was going to make for an awfully long and tense weekend.

Griff parked and honked. They both stared at the front door, but it did not open. Griff honked again, then looked over at Robin.

"No way," Robin said. She was not going to get out of the truck and get even wetter than she already was.

Suddenly, the house door opened and Zo-Zo, dressed in a sun-yellow slicker, ran towards the truck. Griff reached past Robin and pushed open the door.

Zo-Zo stopped abruptly, despite the rain. "I didn't know *you* were coming."

"Griff made me." The rain pelted in through the open door.

Griff waved one arm frantically. "Get in! Before we all get soaked."

Robin shoved her body over and Zo-Zo climbed in. Robin could smell the wet plastic of Zo-Zo's raincoat.

Griff pulled away from the curb and drove on. She was silent for a long time. They all were. But the feeling in the cab of the truck was far from quiet. Robin could almost hear everybody's thoughts buzzing around. Like hornets.

Griff cleared her throat. "I don't play the sergeant-major often, but I want you both to let go of all your hard feelings and have a good time, okay? You can pick up your upset with each other the moment we get back if you want, but let it go for now."

Neither Robin nor Zo-Zo said anything.

"I'll take your silence as agreement," Griff said. Then she began to catch Zo-Zo up on what had been happening at The Wild Place. She didn't mention McCoy once.

After she'd run through the various animals they'd admitted and released, she said, "You haven't missed much. But you've been missed. The place isn't the same without you."

Zo-Zo shifted in her seat, but said nothing.

"So, that's our news," Griff said. "What about you? I hear you're doing a Global Warming project at school. What's your topic?"

"Fracking."

"Fracking," Griff repeated. "Fracking gives me the willies. All those chemicals being shot into the earth to create fractures …"

"Over six hundred chemicals sometimes —" Zo-Zo said.

Griff made a clicking sound with her tongue. "And aren't some of those chemicals linked to cancer?"

As Griff and Zo-Zo talked about fracking, Robin thought about McCoy. She replayed the things they'd talked about and relived some of their special moments, like the time he'd put his arm around her. Remembering these moments made her feel warm and happy. Then, as usual, her mind started to have a few imaginings, like McCoy holding her hand or even kissing her. These daydreams were delicious. Like eating scoops of ice cream, except the exquisite feelings didn't just erupt in her mouth, they fired off through her whole body.

Did McCoy think about her too? She knew he must, but doubted that he was as obsessed with her as she was with him. Would he miss her this weekend? She hoped so.

"What do you think about fracking, Robin?"

Robin looked at Griff. "Fracking? I don't know, I ..." The truth was she hadn't been listening, but she didn't want to say that. Her phone buzzed.

"Someone's texting me," she said. She bent her head down and held the phone in close. The text was from Sienna. She read it quickly.

Boys might crash C's party. Too bad u can't b here.

"Oh, no!" Robin whispered. Panic seized her. What if McCoy was one of the boys that crashed the party? What if Brittany made a play for him? What if —

"Robin, what's wrong?"

Robin didn't look over at Griff. She texted quickly. *What boys?*

"Something's bothering you," Griff said.

"It's nothing," Robin said.

Zo-Zo jumped in. "Probably worried about her *boyfriend*."

"Zo-Zo," Griff warned.

"He's *not* my boyfriend," Robin fired back. He wasn't. Not yet anyway.

"Never will be either. My cousin went to his old school," Zo-Zo said. "Says he picks up girl after girl, then drops them."

Robin felt her chest curl in, as if to protect her heart. She didn't believe it. Zo-Zo was just trying to wreck things. She pressed her back against the seat. Why had she ever agreed to come on this stupid trip anyway?

"Let's change the subject," Griff said. "We're making Robin uneasy."

"She should be uneasy," Zo-Zo said. "She's going to get *decimated*!"

"You don't know that," Griff said quietly. "Robin's smart. She'll figure things out." She pointed out the window. "Look, there's the CN tower. We're almost there. What do you want to do first? Check out those stores on Queen Street or get something to eat?"

"Food first," Zo-Zo said. "I'm starving."

Robin said nothing. She couldn't stop repeating the word "decimated."

"What about you, Robin?" Griff asked. "What do you want to do?"

I want to go home. Knowing this wasn't an option, she hunched her head down into her body. She wished she could be a turtle and crawl into a safe shell. Why wasn't Sienna answering her?

Realizing Griff was still waiting for an answer, she said. "I don't care." And she didn't. It all sucked.

They parked the car at the hotel, checked in, and started walking down the street to find a restaurant. Colours, smells, sounds barraged her. Cars honked, radios blared, trolleys screeched, trucks thundered by. There were people selling jewellery and books and other things from makeshift tables set up along the curbs and she passed people of every skin colour and every possible clothing style. One woman was covered from head to foot in what looked like a box, except it was made out of cloth and had a small mesh window to peer out. To Robin, it looked as if the woman was walking around in her own little closet.

There was so much to look at that soon she became engrossed in the hubbub of the city. The posters particularly fascinated her. They advertised films, yoga classes, political rallies, lost children, and they covered every available surface — telephone poles, billboards, and store windows.

She glanced at them as she went by. Then, something familiar caught her eye and she stopped in front of one in particular. She studied it for a moment, then shouted to her grandmother and Zo-Zo, who had wandered ahead.

"Hey, Griff! Isn't this that friend of yours? Look." She waved them towards her.

All three of them stared at the poster. The banner had big white lettering at the top and said, "SAVE THE WHALES." Beneath that was a picture of a man with salt-and-pepper hair and penetrating eyes.

The face wasn't familiar, but the name written in bold letters underneath was. She pointed to it now and read it aloud.

"Finn Rapier. Isn't that the guy you told me about?"

Griff's hand flew to her mouth. Her fingers moved over her lips as a smile played there. "He looks just the same. Just as handsome."

"You know this guy?" Zo-Zo asked. "I've read about him. He's, like, famous."

"We went to school together," Griff said.

Robin heard something different in her grandmother's voice, something she'd never heard before. It was a kind of yearning.

"Wow." Zo-Zo leaned forward to read the poster. "Look, he's giving a talk."

Robin groaned. The next thing Zo-Zo would be saying was that she wanted to go. And Robin might not get to the t-shirt store she had hoped to go to. She had set her mind on buying McCoy a t-shirt with a wolf on the front.

"Probably happened weeks ago —" Griff said.

"Says the fifteenth," Zo-Zo read. "That's today, isn't it? At 2:30. Convocation Hall."

"That's just around the corner," Griff said. "But it will have started, it —"

"All the better," Zo-Zo said. "We won't have to wait."

Griff turned to Robin. "I know you wanted to find that t-shirt store."

Zo-Zo waved away the concern as if it were a housefly. "We can do that after. Come on, let's go. Or we'll miss even more of it." She started walking.

"Wait, it's this way," Griff said. She took Zo-Zo's arm and linked it through hers and the two of them strode off.

Robin followed sulkily. Zo-Zo was being as pushy as ever.

CHAPTER
TEN

When they entered the hall, it took Robin's eyes a few minutes to adjust to the darkness. When they did, she could see that all the seats were taken, so she stood beside Griff and Zo-Zo and leaned against the back wall. Huge images of whales filled the screen up on the stage.

A tall, athletic man with gun-grey hair was standing beside the screen. From the picture on the poster, Robin guessed it was Finn Rapier. He was good looking for an older man, she thought. And agile, moving around the stage with great energy and enthusiasm.

"That's my boat, the *Sea Serpent*," Finn said, clicking a new photograph onto the screen. His eyes glinted with pride.

Robin didn't know much about boats — she'd never been in anything bigger than a speed boat — but this one was large and painted blue and grey in a kind of camouflage pattern. Its flag had a skull and crossbones on it.

The picture on the screen changed and now showed a much larger boat, with the word "Research" painted in huge letters on the side. "And this is a Japanese whaling boat. The *Hanta-kira*. The one I was telling you about."

"It calls itself a 'Research' boat because it's legal to kill whales for scientific investigation. But believe me, scientific investigation is a far cry from what this boat actually does. I'll warn you, the next few photographs are not for the squeamish."

A new picture appeared on the screen. It was of a large whale with a spear sticking out of its side. A huge circle of blood stained the water around it.

"Gross," Zo-Zo whispered.

The next slide showed a whale being pulled up into the ship via a large ramp.

"We radioed the *Hanta-kira* and told them they were in a whale sanctuary and contravening international law, but they didn't care. They knew all that anyway. They were there to kill whales and that's what they were doing. So we decided to stop them. The only way to do that was to ram their ship with our ship."

"This guy is *amazing!*" Zo-Zo said. Her voice was full of reverence.

Robin stared at the screen. Was he really going to ram the other boat? What if it sunk? What if people were killed? Wide-eyed, she stared at the next few slides.

"Here's us giving their boat a little nudge. Just enough to disable the spear gun," Finn said.

The picture on the screen showed the broken spear gun dangling from the front of the research boat.

"Then we told them to leave the area again, but they didn't seem to hear us. So we gave them a bigger nudge, just to show them we meant business."

A photograph of the *Sea Serpent* bashing into the side of the Japanese boat appeared on the screen.

"Whoa," Zo-Zo said in a low voice.

"I'll never forget the look on the captain's face when we bashed his boat. He looked like he was going to pee his pants." Finn grinned. "I guess he didn't expect us to actually do it."

"Awesome!" Zo-Zo cried. The word shot out into the crowd and a ripple of laughter went through the audience.

Finn smiled as he peered into the crowd. "I seem to have an exuberant fan back there." He swept his fingers through his thick hair and clicked to another slide. This one was a picture of the research boat's back end.

"Finally the *Hanta-kira* got our message and scuttled back to Japan. With a few dents and one demolished spear gun."

The crowd clapped wildly. Robin joined in the applause. What Finn was doing was inspiring. She wished McCoy was here. He would have loved it. Besides, it would have saved her from worrying about him going to that stupid party. As the applause started to wane, hands shot up.

Finn pointed to Zo-Zo, who was pogo-sticking her arm in the air, making it go as high as she could. "Okay, Miss Exuberance, fire away."

Zo-Zo rose up on her tiptoes. "What do you tell people who say you shouldn't break the law to save the environment?"

He smiled. It was obviously a question he was asked often.

"Remember, what these whaling boats are doing is *illegal*. They were in an actual *whale sanctuary*."

"But when you hit the other boat, you were damaging property," someone in the audience shouted out.

Finn nodded as if he'd heard these concerns a hundred times.

"If you saw someone hurting a child, you'd stop them. Or try to. Any decent person would. Because it's the right thing to do." His eyes became intense and insistent. "It's no different with whales. We have to take action *NOW.* Or there won't be any whales left. That's what people have to understand. The time for being nice is over. *OVER!*"

A few people clapped loudly and cheered.

There were several other questions and finally, a man wearing a t-shirt with a whale on the front came forward and told the crowd that Mr. Rapier would now be signing books for those who wanted to purchase them.

"Thanks, Leon," Finn said, leaving the stage to even more applause. He walked over to a long table which had been set up in the corner and contained a stack of books and t-shirts.

Robin checked her phone. Still no message from Sienna. *McCoy wouldn't crash a party, would he?* Slipping her phone back in her pocket, she counted her money. She couldn't afford to buy McCoy a wolf t-shirt and whale t-shirt, so she was going to have to decide.

"Think I'll get one of those shirts for my mom," Zo-Zo said, moving towards the line. "If I have enough money, I'll buy the book too." She turned to Griff. "Come on, stand in line with me. I want to see if he remembers you."

Robin looked at her grandmother. She had a shy, uncertain look on her face. Griff, shy? Who'd have thought?

Zo-Zo tugged Griff's sleeve and pulled her into the line. "How do you know him anyway? From high school?"

"He was her boyfriend," Robin said.

"Your *boyfriend!* Finn Rapier was your *boyfriend?*"

"Sh!" Griff turned away from the people who were turning to stare at her. "It's a long story."

"Tell me," Zo-Zo said.

"Maybe on the way home."

Zo-Zo stomped her foot. "No! I can't wait that long."

"You're going to have to," Griff said.

Robin moved in place behind them. She'd made up her mind now. She was going to buy the t-shirt with the picture of the whale soaring out of the water. She'd find a wolf t-shirt another time.

They paid for their purchases and waited for the line to take them to Finn, who was signing things up ahead. The line moved slowly, but suddenly, the person ahead stepped away and there was Finn, sitting at a desk in front of them.

Zo-Zo pressed her book forward.

Finn took it and looked up at her.

"Ah, Miss Exuberance." His face was full of merriment and warmth. "My kind of person."

"Can you dedicate my book to someone?" she asked him.

"Sure." He opened the book to the title page. "Fire away...." He readied his pen, waiting for Zo-Zo to say a name.

"To Griff."

His black, bristly eyebrows bashed together in confusion and he raised his eyes.

"Griff!?"

His thrust his chair back and moved quickly around the table, then wrapped his arms around Griff in a deep, all-embracing hug.

Robin and Zo-Zo exchanged a look and giggled.

"It's been so long," he said, as he moved to hold Griff at arm's length. His face was flushed, his eyes gleaming.

He glanced at Zo-Zo and Robin. "These must be your grandchildren —"

Griff put her arm around Robin. "This is my granddaughter, Robin."

"Robin!" He took both her hands in his and pumped them up and down with unabashed exuberance. "How wonderful to meet you."

Robin smiled. She found his dog-like friendliness hard to resist.

Griff put her other arm around Zo-Zo. "And this is Zo-Zo, Robin's best friend."

Finn was shaking Zo-Zo's hand when Leon interrupted.

"Mr. Rapier. Perhaps your friends could wait at the side while you sign the rest of the books. There are only a few people left —"

"Oh, yes, of course." He turned back to Griff. "Don't go away. I'll be as quick as I can."

Griff nodded.

While they waited, they leafed through the various pamphlets on the table. Robin was impressed. Finn was a lot more than a one-man whale saving operation. He'd created a whole organization to help him.

"Just goes to show you the difference one person can make," Griff said, scanning the table. "He'll be impressed when I tell him about The Wild Place and all the animals you two have saved."

Zo-Zo looked dubious. "But what Finn's doing is *huge!*"

"I know, but remember, it all started with one animal. And it grew from there. If you two keep at it, you'll be environmental heroes just like he is."

Robin gave Zo-Zo a wide-eyed grin and laughed. *Was that possible? Really?*

"Don't look so surprised," Griff said. "Together, you two have made a big difference to animals in our area."

Griff had emphasized the word "together" and now it flashed like a neon sign, pulsing in the air between them. Robin could feel the brightness of it dispelling the tension she'd felt towards Zo-Zo for months.

Finn appeared, put his arms around them and herded them towards the door.

"Let's get something to eat. There's a great Thai restaurant just down the street. I'm starved."

Inside the restaurant, they had just settled themselves around a large round table when a waiter appeared.

"The usual, Mr. Finn?"

"Not today," he said. "I don't want one thing that's 'usual.'" He laughed. "Today is special. So bring out your specials. Every single one of them."

"But no fish, right?"

"No. No fish." He turned to his companions. "I don't eat fish."

Robin liked hearing that. Here was a guy who walked his talk.

"Are you vegan?" Zo-Zo asked.

"On the boat, yes," he said. "But sometimes out here

I let myself have a —"

"Don't tell me," Griff said. "A bacon sandwich." They both laughed.

Robin listened while the two of them reminisced about their school days in Toronto.

"You lived in Toronto?" Robin asked. This surprised her. Griff seemed like such an outdoors person.

"Yup. For a few years. Back then, where we live now was just a cottage."

"Good thing or I wouldn't have met you," Finn said.

Robin watched as Griff and Finn talked. Her grandmother's face was full of life and she was giggling. Giggling. That wasn't something Robin had heard her do very often. She was fiddling with her hair too.

The waiter appeared and placed several platters of food on the table, then lifted the metal covers. Steam and the aroma of spicy, cooked vegetables blossomed into the air.

"Dig in everyone!" Finn said.

Robin took a little from the closest plate and tasted it, then reached for her water glass. Her mouth was on fire.

"Should have told you about that one," Finn said. "Or given you a fire extinguisher." His face erupted with laughter. "What can I say? I like food hot!"

"You like everything hot," Griff said.

Robin saw Griff and Finn's eyes lock. Their faces blushed. Robin turned to Zo-Zo and they both smirked.

They finished all the food on the platters, then Finn ordered some desserts, then more desserts. The meal was going on for hours. As they ate, Zo-Zo asked Finn more questions and got him talking. Finn liked Zo-Zo, Robin could tell. Everyone liked Zo-Zo. She was so outgoing and so much easier to get to know than she was. Which made it all the more remarkable that McCoy had chosen her over Zo-Zo. And all the more important that she keep him. She checked her phone again. Frustrated that she still hadn't heard from Sienna, she texted McCoy himself now. As they lingered over desserts, then tea, Robin waited for him to reply, but he didn't. That worried her. What was going on? She checked her watch. It was almost eight o'clock. Soon Caitlyn's party was going to start. Would McCoy be one of the boys to crash it? It was hard to relax when the boy she adored might be with a bunch of girls who were going to do everything they could to steal him away.

Griff put her fork down. "Goodness, I haven't had such a wonderful dinner in years. The pad thai was fabulous."

"It was." He turned to the girls. "As you no doubt know, your grandmother is an excellent cook herself. If only I had someone as good on the *Sea Serpent*. 'Specially right now. My usual cook has had to go back to Australia to face some immigration issues."

He lifted his teacup, then set it down with a clatter. "I've just had the most incredible idea." He shook his head and shrugged, not taking his eyes away from Griff. "Look, I know it's crazy, but my life has been built on crazy, so I'm going to say it anyway." He wet his full lips. "Why don't you come on the ship for a few weeks? Be our cook."

Griff stared at him, momentarily speechless.

"It would be one heck of a holiday. You'd get to see all the whales and dolphins and sharks you could ever imagine, all in exchange for cooking a few meals —"

Zo-Zo leapt out of her chair. "Do it, Griff, do it."

"I couldn't. The girls and I, we run a wild animal shelter, we —"

Robin stood up too, speaking quickly. "There's hardly any animals in the wintertime. Nothing Laura, Dad, and the two of us can't handle." She looked at Zo-Zo, who nodded vigorously.

"Think about it," Finn said. "Wouldn't be for a few weeks anyway. I've got this pesky court case in Iceland to deal with, but I'll be heading out to the Southern Ocean right after that. Please come."

Griff scrunched up her face. "And see whales get killed? I don't think I could stand to see that."

"That Japanese whaling boat wouldn't dare show up again this year. Not after what we did to it last year. I don't expect any trouble."

Zo-Zo started bouncing on her toes. "I wish I could go. I LOVE whales."

Finn's eyebrows jumped up into his forehead as if they were getting out of the way of something. "Since I'm already going crazy here, I might as well go the whole way. Why don't you all come?"

Zo-Zo jerked her head towards Griff. "Oh, Griff, please say 'yes.' Please. My dad would let me do it, I know he would. It's a chance of a lifetime, it's …"

Robin felt her whole body buzzing. This would be an adventure to end all adventures. She'd get to go on a plane, something she hadn't done before, she'd get to see Australia, a whole new country, and best of all, she'd get a chance to experience whales. Whales! And they're would be all kinds of other marine life to see too!

Images floated up into her mind like shiny air bubbles. Almost as soon as they appeared, however, fear-thoughts dive-bombed them, shooting them down. What if her plane crashed? Or the boat sank? Or McCoy fell in love with Brittany while she was away?

Feeling as if she were in the middle of a war video game, she shifted her attention to Griff's face. Would Griff even consider letting them go? Robin didn't think so. They would be away for weeks. What about school?

Finn laughed. "It's a crazy idea, I know."

Griff put her hand over her mouth as if trying to control the huge smile that was forming there and looked at the girls. "He loves crazy. Always has."

Finn laughed. "Crazy gets a bad rap. If you ask me, we need a lot *more* crazy. Crazy is the wild side. It's wilderness and all the things I love. Show me someone who's willing to be crazy, and I'll show you someone who has courage. Real courage."

Zo-Zo threw her arms out to the side of her body, her fingers curled and her thumbs pointing straight up. Her face gushed with happiness.

"When are we leaving?"

CHAPTER
ELEVEN

After they'd said goodbye to Finn, the three of them walked around downtown for a while, looking at the store windows. The air was cold and the stars were bright, but the streets were still busy with people rushing this way and that. Robin looked at their faces, but no one looked at her or even acknowledged her existence. She always experienced that when she came to the city.

As they wandered around, Zo-Zo talked incessantly about the whale expedition, rattling off reason after reason why Griff should let them do it.

"The biggest reason," Zo-Zo said, "is that whales are in trouble. If we go, we could take pictures and do presentations when we come back. Right Robin?"

Robin nodded as she suppressed a yawn. She was tired, tired of waiting for her phone to ring, tired of imagining what might be happening at Caitlyn's party and tired from all the walking they'd done today. It didn't help that her mind kept creating pictures of Brittany and McCoy kissing. If only she could unscrew her head and dump it in one of the garbage bins she saw along the sidewalk.

It was late when they got back to the hotel and they all changed into their pyjamas. Griff had a bath and Zo-Zo began flicking through the TV channels.

Robin couldn't stop thinking about Caitlyn's party. It would be in full swing by now, which meant there'd be little hope of anyone texting her. Everyone would be too busy having a good time. Everyone but her. If only she could be there.

"Wouldn't it be amazing if we *did* go to the Southern Ocean and we *did* run into that Japanese whaling boat?" Zo-Zo said.

Griff stepped out of the bathroom and pulled the sash of her bath robe tight. "If we go, and I'm not saying we are, we're not getting involved in any high-seas, whale-saving war. That's *NOT* what this trip is about."

Zo-Zo gave Griff a pleading look. "I can always dream, can't I?"

"The two of you are far too young for such shenanigans. It would be far too dangerous. I wouldn't even consider going if I felt there was a likelihood of seeing the Japanese boat." She unwound her braid of hair from where she'd pinned it to the top of her head.

"Finn said that's not going to happen," Zo-Zo reminded her. "Besides, think of all the amazing wildlife we'd see down there. Kangaroos, whales, penguins — it would be awesome."

A wistful look crossed Griff's face. "I must admit, I'd love to see kangaroos." She smiled at Robin. "And whales."

Robin tried to imagine what it would be like to see a real, live whale. Her mind flashed back to some of the pictures in Finn's presentation. The idea of being up close with an animal a hundred times her size was both thrilling and scary.

"We could even do a video about our trip," Zo-Zo said. "Call it 'The Wild Place on the Road' or something. Maybe it would go viral. Think of all the publicity we'd get for whales then!"

Griff turned to Zo-Zo. "Does that mean you're going to start helping out at The Wild Place again?"

Zo-Zo's eyes were on the TV, but she bobbed her head up and down in a fervent "yes." She clicked away at the remote control. "Look, there's a movie about a girl and a whale. *Whale Rider*. How cool is that? Can we watch it?"

Griff nodded and they settled in. The movie was about a Maori girl who had been denied leadership because of her gender. As the girl learned to ride whales, however, she was able to gain the respect of her community.

Robin was so gripped by the story that she almost didn't hear her phone buzz. She read the text from Sienna quickly.

Boys just crashed C's. What a blast!

Robin texted back right away. *Is McCoy there?*

She waited for a reply, but none came. So she texted again. Still no reply. Keeping her phone close at hand, she tried to watch the film, but it was hard to concentrate.

Finally, Griff said, "Come on, Robin, put that phone aside for a while. Nothing earth shaking is going to happen in just a few hours."

Oh yeah? How do you know? Robin set aside her phone, but after several minutes, she couldn't stand it and snuck into the washroom to see if any messages had come in. None had. What was going on?

When she went back in, Griff pulled her over and began rubbing her shoulders.

"You seem so wound up tonight. Is everything okay?" Griff asked.

Robin shrugged. She might have told Griff if Zo-Zo hadn't been there, but she didn't want to give Zo-Zo the satisfaction of knowing she was worrying about McCoy liking someone else. What Zo-Zo had said in the car about McCoy being a heart breaker still grated in her mind.

"Come on, breathe," Griff encouraged. "You're not taking in enough oxygen to keep a mosquito alive."

Robin made herself take a long breath. It was hard. Her chest felt tight and constricted. But Griff's hands were warm and soothing and she felt herself starting to relax. As she did, she pretended that Griff's hands belonged to McCoy. That felt really good. Until she started imagining McCoy massaging Brittany's shoulders.

"I don't know what you're thinking about," Griff said, "But change the channel."

Robin frowned. She didn't know how to change the channel. Her phone buzzed. "I *have* to get this."

Griff moved away. Robin turned and read the text. *McCoy's drinking beer!*

Alarmed, Robin fell back against the pillows. *McCoy was there? And drinking beer?* There had never been beer at any party she'd gone to before. For all she knew, Brittany might be too. The idea of McCoy, Brittany, and beer all being in the same place at the same time felt disastrous. And she could do nothing about it. *Nothing.* She wanted to throw her phone out the window.

The film ended, but Robin felt too discombobulated to take in what was happening.

Griff yawned. "I'm going to hit the hay. I want to get up early so we don't miss Zo-Zo's mom. I wouldn't want her going out before we get there."

Right. Zo-Zo's mom. Robin had completely forgotten that they were going to visit her first thing in the morning. She wished they could just go back. The sooner she could find out what had happened at the party, the better.

"My mom never gets up early," Zo-Zo said. "At least she never did when she lived with me and Dad. Besides, Derek, the guy she lives with, he won't like it if we wake him up."

Zo-Zo said the word "Derek" as if it were a bit of bad tasting food. "He's not going to like us just showing up either. He *hates* it when people stop by."

"You tried to call," Robin said. She felt irritated at this stupid Derek guy, irritated at Caitlyn for having her stupid party, and irritated at Griff for making her miss it.

"I did more than call," Zo-Zo said. "I texted, I emailed, I did *everything* I could. For three whole weeks."

"Of course you did," Griff said.

Zo-Zo's next words were spoken softly, almost pleadingly. "I just need to know she's okay."

"Of course you do." Griff turned out the light by her bed. "I'm sure she'll be delighted to see you."

"I hope so," Zo-Zo said, but Robin could hear the uncertainty in her voice.

"Once before, I couldn't get her for seventeen days," Zo-Zo whispered. It was like she was telling a secret. "She'd been drinking."

Robin felt a wrenching in her chest. It would be so hard to have a parent with a drinking problem. She thought about Brodie and what he'd told her about his dad going on drinking binges and then yelling at him. It was awful. Robin couldn't remember Zo-Zo ever saying anything about her mom getting drunk and screaming at her, but nonetheless, she had the impression that drinking was more important to Zo-Zo's mom than Zo-Zo was. Robin's chest filled with sadness for her friend. It was one thing to have your mother *taken away,* but to have your mother *choose* to be away — that had to hurt.

"Does her partner Derek drink a lot too?" Griff asked.

"Like a fish," Zo-Zo said.

"Don't insult the fish," Robin said matter-of-factly.

Zo-Zo burst out laughing. Zo-Zo's laughter got Robin laughing, which made Zo-Zo laugh more, then Robin laughed more too and soon they were both doubled over on the huge king-sized bed laughing until tears were streaming down their faces.

Griff regarded them happily. "Reminds me of the good old days."

"Yeah," Zo-Zo said and went to brush her teeth.

Robin brushed her teeth too, then climbed under the covers on one side of the bed. She was tired, very tired, and thought she'd fall asleep right away. They'd closed the curtains, but light barged in around the edges of the window like a burglar. Even though it was late, Robin could still hear screeching tires, cars honking, and sirens wailing. How was she ever going to sleep?

On the far side of the bed, Zo-Zo tossed and turned. Robin guessed she was probably worried about the visit with her mom tomorrow. Robin stared at the ceiling and wondered which was worse, having a mother who had died, like she did, or having a mother who lived in another city with someone she didn't like. She knew the answer in a heartbeat — it was better to have a mother who was alive. A thousand times better. No, a *million* times better.

But her mother wasn't alive. She was gone. *Gone.* Robin still found that hard to believe sometimes. How could someone be in your life for years and years and then no longer be in your life? Robin couldn't wrap her mind around it. And now, she had to face the fact that McCoy might not be in her life anymore either. If he became Brittany's boyfriend, he would sit beside *her* on the bus, be with *her* at lunch, and do things with *her* after school. Robin would be forced to see them together each and every day. It would all be right in front of her face.

She shut her eyes tight. She mustn't let that happen. She didn't think she could stand it.

CHAPTER TWELVE

The next morning, Robin checked her phone before she got out of bed. Nothing. No text, no email, nothing. Was that because no one wanted to deliver the bad news that McCoy and Brittany were now together? Probably.

Robin winced. She'd lost him. She was sure of it.

Rolling over, she pulled the pillow over her head. She did not want to get up. She did not want to face this day. Beside her Zo-Zo groaned and yawned, but pushed herself up. Eventually, Robin did too and trudged behind Zo-Zo and Griff as they made their way to the dining room for breakfast. Robin felt as if she were wading through a sea of wet cement.

In the hotel restaurant, Griff picked a table in the corner and they all sat down. Robin looked at Zo-Zo. There were puffy little pillows under her eyes and she didn't look as if she'd slept. One knee, however, was jittering up and down.

"Nervous?" Griff asked her.

Zo-Zo swallowed hard. "I have a bad feeling about this."

Robin expected Griff to tell Zo-Zo that everything would be fine. That's what adults usually did. But Griff leaned over, put her arm around Zo-Zo and squeezed her shoulders. "Whatever happens, we'll face it together."

The waiter came to take their order.

"I'm not hungry," Zo-Zo said.

Robin didn't bother even opening the menu. She felt too depressed to eat.

The nests of lines surrounding Griff's eyes deepened. "Bring them each a cup of hot milk. I'll have some scrambled eggs. Free-range eggs, of course." A smile played on her lips.

The waiter frowned. "Free-range? I don't think we have free-range eggs —"

"Send over the manager," Griff said.

Robin and Zo-Zo exchanged a she's-going-to-embarrass-us look and the waiter scuttled off.

Griff gave them an amused smile. "I'm feeling frisky this morning."

The manager came over and Griff gave him a short speech about why using free-range eggs was important.

"It would make you cry to see the conditions these factory-farmed chickens are raised in," she told him.

Robin studied the man. He didn't look like the kind of person who would cry over cruelty to chickens, or anything else for that matter, but he was acting like he was, nodding in agreement to everything Griff said.

When Griff was finished, the manager left and she turned to the girls. "Who knows? Maybe the next time the guy's in a grocery store, he'll pick up some free-range eggs and try them out. Once he does, he'll be hooked. And then he'll eat them on his organic, genetically unmodified whole wheat bread! Ha!" She laughed loudly at herself.

Zo-Zo looked up at the ceiling.

"Mock me if you want." Griff smiled. "Just trying to spread the word."

Robin did her best chicken imitation. *Bok, bok, bok, bok, bok.*

A smile wobbled around Zo-Zo's lips, but Griff laughed out loud. As if Robin had just said the funniest thing.

Robin and Zo-Zo exchanged a look. What was going on?

The waiter delivered the cups of milk and a plate of eggs. He kept his eyes averted and did not look at any of them.

Griff raised her fork with gusto. "I don't know why I'm so hungry this morning, but I could eat a horse. Figuratively speaking, of course." She laughed again.

Robin yawned. Sometimes she appreciated Griff's dedication to being cheerful, other times, it was just downright annoying. Like this morning.

Griff ate a forkful of eggs and made a face. "These eggs taste like mushy cardboard." She patted her lips with a napkin and opened her large cotton bag. "This will help." She unscrewed a small bottle of maple syrup and drooled a stream of it over her eggs, then ate another forkful. "Much better."

"Is that the stuff you guys make?" Zo-Zo asked.

Griff nodded. "It's like a little bit of home in a bottle." She added some to each cup of hot milk.

Robin sipped it. She had to admit, it tasted good.

When breakfast was done, Griff wrapped her arms around their shoulders and led them down to the underground parking lot. Soon they were making their way through the city. Even though it was early, the air had a smoky, gritty smell to it. Robin glowered out her window. Did anyone here even remember what fresh air smelled like? If a person was born in the city and grew up here, they wouldn't even know what clean air smelled like. How could they?

Everywhere she looked, it was grey. Grey sky, grey roads, grey buildings. As they drove through some residential streets to get to the highway, the roads were littered with blackened, dead leaves. Robin shivered. It was a cold, wet morning and Robin wondered why Griff didn't put the heat on.

Griff rolled down her window. "What a beautiful day! The air's so fresh!"

"What's beautiful about it?" Robin stared at the sky. The clouds were low, their purple bellies plump with rain. Rain that looked as if it was about to dump itself on the world. Couldn't Griff see that?

"You're in an awfully bad mood." Griff said softly. "What's up?"

I got no sleep last night. I've probably lost the only boy I care about. And I'm spending the day doing something I don't want to do — pick one! She pressed her lips together and rolled them back into her mouth. If she spoke, she'd just make matters worse.

Griff began to whistle and Robin gritted her teeth. Why was Griff in such a good mood? Was this because of Finn? It had to be. Now she felt even more irritated.

Weren't people her grandmother's age supposed to be finished with crushes on boys?

They drove and drove. Soon they were in a rundown area on the city's outskirts. As they passed small, box-like houses looking for the right one, Robin could feel the tension in the car rising. By the time Griff pulled the car slowly to a halt, she could barely pull air into her lungs.

The house had dirty white siding and some bags of garbage piled up outside. Some dogs must have gotten into them as plastic wrappers and empty food tins were strewn around the yard.

"Is this the place?" Griff asked.

"She would have cleaned up if she knew we were coming," Zo-Zo said.

"Of course she would have." Griff turned off the engine. The quiet pounded into Robin's ears.

Griff spoke gently to Zo-Zo. "How do you want to handle this? Do you want to go up to the door alone? Do you want me or Robin to come? You're in charge, but we're here to support you in whatever way you want us to."

"I'll go by myself," Zo-Zo said and reached for the door handle.

Robin eyed the rundown house. What kind of people would live in a place like that?

Zo-Zo turned her head towards Robin. "Will you come?"

Cringing, Robin followed Zo-Zo up the walkway. There were bits of broken glass scattered over the cracked paving stones. They crunched under her feet.

When they go to the door, Zo-Zo pressed the bell. It made no ringing sound.

"I don't think it's working," Robin said.

Zo-Zo rapped on the door with her bare knuckles.

No one came.

She's not there, Robin was about to say. Good, now they could go home.

"She's in there, I know she is," Zo-Zo said. She knocked again. Harder. Then harder still. Robin turned to look at Griff, who was watching them from the van. What should they do?

As Robin turned back to the door, it opened a few inches. A man with wild eyes appeared in the opening, spikes of his hair lunging out every which way. He was wearing a torn undershirt and boxer shorts.

"What the f—" He looked back and forth between Robin and Zo-Zo.

Even though Robin wasn't standing close, she could smell the beer and cigarettes on his breath and see the helter-skelter of little red veins in his milky eyes.

"Derek," Zo-Zo said.

His expression remained sour. "What do you want?"

The door opened wider and a woman Robin assumed was Zo-Zo's mother appeared, clutching a faded house-coat at the throat. Her fingers were bone thin and white.

"Zoey. My girl!" Her eyes were watery and red and she reached out and brushed the back of her hand against Zo-Zo's cheek.

"Jesus!" The man bolted back angrily and disappeared inside the house. He whacked the door so that it hit the back of Zo-Zo's mom.

"Mom!"

"Don't mind him. He's just in a bad mood. What are you doing here? Is everything all right?"

"Mom, I've been phoning and phoning, I've been worried —"

Zo-Zo's mom lowered her voice. "We're a bit behind right now on the bills, the phone —"

"I've got money." Zo-Zo pulled some bills from her pocket. "Take it, I —"

"Take it!" the man shouted from inside.

"No, I couldn't —"

Derek's arm shot out and he grabbed the money from Zo-Zo's hand.

"Give it back," Griff said.

Robin hadn't seen her grandmother come towards them, but was relieved she was there, standing behind them in her solid, no-nonsense way.

Derek appeared in the doorway again, stiff and indignant. "Who's gonna make me? You?"

"I'm sure I could get the police to assist me. I'll call them right now and have you charged with theft."

Derek sneered. "You don't scare me."

Zo-Zo's mom eased the money out of his grasp slowly, as if expecting his hand to rise up and slap her. She tried to give it back to Zo-Zo, but Zo-Zo shook her head.

"Pay the phone bill, mom. Then I can call you."

"I will sweetheart, I will." She crumpled the bills hard against her chest, as if trying to make them disappear behind her ribcage where Derek could not get them.

Griff looked beseechingly at Zo-Zo's mom. "Would you come out with us for a coffee? So you can visit with Zo-Zo?"

"She's not leaving this frigging house."

He said the words so forcefully, that Robin stepped back. She could feel Griff's chest against her spine and was grateful for it.

Zo-Zo's mother closed her eyes. When she opened them again, they were full of tears.

Derek turned away. "Get them out of here! Now!"

"I'd better go," Zo-Zo's mother said. Her face agonized, she shut the door slowly, as if she were pressing a pillow into a child's suffocating face.

CHAPTER
THIRTEEN

At school on Monday, the rumours about what had happened the night of Caitlyn's party were snapping like sparks out of a bonfire. Each rumour soared through the darkness in Robin's mind, bright and burning. If she thought about one too long, or started to believe it, the heat from it singed her like a smoking cinder.

One rumour claimed that McCoy and some other boys had snuck into Caitlyn's house with a case of beer. Another was that Caitlyn's father had chased them all away. The rumour that burned the hottest had Brittany and McCoy making out in a corner.

Robin didn't know what to believe and she walked into her classroom stiff with apprehension, half expecting to see McCoy and Brittany huddled together. McCoy, however, was sitting at his desk, chatting to the boy beside him, but he smiled warmly at her and she stared to relax. Nothing seemed different. It was the same at lunch. There was some general talk about the party, but the questions that were smoldering in Robin's mind went unanswered. She'd have to wait until after school to ask them. *That's IF he comes to The Wild Place and doesn't go to Brittany's,* a voice inside her said. Even though everything seemed the same, she still felt uncertain.

When he climbed into the bus and sat beside her on the way home, Robin felt relieved and started to tell him about Finn and the whale presentation.

"The guy sounds cool," McCoy said.

"He wants to take Griff, Zo-Zo, and me on a whale expedition to the Southern Ocean in a couple of weeks."

"No way!" He studied her face. "You don't sound very excited."

She *was* excited. Part of her wanted to jump up and down and start packing. This trip, even the possibility of it, was the most exciting thing that had ever happened to her. Yet she was afraid. She had worried herself sick over McCoy this last weekend. How was she going to handle being away for weeks?

"My dad would never let me do something like that. Not if it meant missing school."

"Griff would make us take school work with us. Besides, she says it would be the education of a lifetime. We'd be gone for almost a month."

She wanted him to say, *But that's so long.* Or, *I'd miss you.* Something. Anything. But he didn't. Why didn't he? Was he just not the type to say such things or had something happened at the party to make him no longer care? She had to find out.

They got off the bus, greeted the dogs that ran out to meet them, and walked past the barn to the area where they were building the wolf enclosure. All the posts had already been dug in so their job now was to attach the chain fencing. Together they unravelled the roll and Robin held the fencing in place while McCoy fastened it. She was inches away from him, so close that she could feel the warmth of his body.

She waited until some of the fencing was up, then, keeping her voice casual, said, "How was the party?"

Confusion rumpled his face. "What party?"

"Caitlyn's."

"I wouldn't call that a party. Just a bunch of girls. Tom likes Caitlyn so he wanted to crash it. I went along."

McCoy unrolled more of the fencing.

Sounds innocent enough, Robin thought. She waited for him to say more, but he didn't. She didn't want to interrogate him, but she'd go crazy if she didn't get more specific details.

"Someone said you were drinking beer. With Brittany." There, she'd said it.

"We passed around the one can we found in the bar fridge." McCoy said, frowning. His voice sounded irritated. "Then Caitlyn's dad came out and chased us off."

So, nothing had happened. Nothing at all. Robin felt herself starting to settle down.

When they were finished, she ran to the house and came back with the t-shirt she'd bought at Finn's talk and handed it to him.

He held it up and nodded approvingly, then pulled off the t-shirt he was wearing.

Robin stared at his arms and shoulders. He was muscular and beautiful.

He pulled the t-shirt over his head and pulled it down just past the waist of his jeans. It fit him perfectly. He spun in place. "Cool."

Robin smiled. It looked wonderful on him.

"Can I borrow your bike to ride home?" he asked.

Robin nodded. Of course. He could have anything of hers. Anything.

"Thanks," he said and hugged her. She felt herself falling into his warmth, his ease, his safety. She wished she could stay there, but he released her and said he had to go. With the new t-shirt still on, he climbed on her bike. It was way too small for him, but she liked that he was going to ride it. It made her feel close to him somehow.

"Nice shirt," Griff called as she and Zo-Zo rounded the corner of the barn.

Robin had known Zo-Zo was going to start working at The Wild Place again, but still, it felt odd. Like two worlds colliding.

McCoy grinned and waved as he pedalled off. Griff went off to finish her chores, ,but Zo-Zo stood in place, squinting at Robin as if she couldn't believe what she was seeing. "You *gave* him that t-shirt? After all that happened at the party?"

"It wasn't a party," Robin said quickly. "And nothing happened."

"Right," Zo-Zo hissed. "And my mom doesn't drink." She stomped off towards the barn.

Robin watched Zo-Zo walk away. Obviously, Zo-Zo was believing the rumours. If Robin hadn't heard the truth from McCoy, she might have believed them too.

From then on, Zo-Zo continued to work at The Wild Place, but she always stuck close to Griff and left

Robin and McCoy to themselves. Robin was grateful for that, but sometimes when she heard Griff and Zo-Zo laughing, she missed her friend. When she and Zo-Zo did talk, the only topic that seemed safe enough was the whale expedition.

"Can't we just buy the tickets to Australia now?" Zo-Zo asked. "Just so we know the trip is going to happen?"

"But we don't know whether the trip's going to happen," Griff said, flicking on the windshield wipers. It was Saturday afternoon and they were all in the van on their way to a mall. Robin had wanted McCoy to come too, but they'd finished the fencing that morning and he'd gone home to do some things for his mom. Since it was sleeting out and Squirm had to get a birthday present for a party, Griff had suggested they all go to the mall.

"We have to wait to see what happens to Finn in Iceland," Griff said. "He may have to spend a few months in jail."

Zo-Zo gasped. "He can't go to jail. He just can't."

"Tell that to the judge," Griff said. "I think the authorities are starting to realize that's the only way to stop him. He's a veritable force, that man."

Zo-Zo bit her lip in frustration. "I want to go on this whale expedition more than I've ever wanted anything."

Squirm made a beak out of his hand and began flapping it open and shut. "So you keep telling us." Robin stared out the window. The sleet was turning to snow. It was the first snow of the season. She liked snow, liked the way the little fluffy balls danced in the air, but she didn't feel ready for it yet. If only there was a way to have the snow without the cold.

She pulled out her phone, snapped a picture of the snow and sent it to McCoy with a short text. She knew she shouldn't text him so much, but she couldn't stop herself. It was just something she *had* to do. The problem was, when he didn't answer, which was most of the time, it just made her want to text him more.

Since the party, she'd become a complete worrywart. Something wasn't right between her and McCoy. She didn't know what it was, or even how to figure out what it was, but something kept nibbling at her peace of mind. It reminded her of a mouse they'd had in the kitchen last year. They could never see it, only guessed it was there by some faint teeth marks in the butter.

Griff looked at Zo-Zo in the rear-view mirror. "Have you heard from your mom?"

Zo-Zo shook her head. "Nope. I'm starting to give up on her."

"I'll drive you down to see her again if you want," Griff said.

Zo-Zo sighed heavily. "If only seeing my mom didn't involve seeing Derek." Robin couldn't imagine how hard it would be if her dad had gotten involved with someone she didn't like. Just seeing her dad put his arm around Laura sometimes, or give her a quick kiss on the cheek, was challenging enough. And she liked Laura.

She looked over at Zo-Zo. Her hair was stringy, as if it hadn't been washed in weeks, and she'd failed a test in geography last week. Robin had never known her to fail a test.

Zo-Zo met her gaze. "If Griff takes me to see her again, will you come?"

Robin looked away. She didn't want to. That would mean giving up her time with McCoy.

Zo-Zo's face reddened and she looked away. "Thanks. Thanks a lot."

"I'll go, I ..."

Zo-Zo's face was hard now, closed and locked like a door. She stared out the window.

Robin felt badly. She wished Zo-Zo understood, but she didn't. Griff didn't understand either. They didn't like McCoy, didn't want her to spend time with him. Just last week, Griff had given her grief about going over to McCoy's place after school instead of coming right home to feed the animals. The animals could wait a few hours, couldn't they? Robin thought so, but Griff was acting like she was shirking her responsibilities.

Griff parked the van and they went inside the mall. They walked around for a while, then Griff parked herself on a bench and let everyone do their own thing. Ari went off to try on jeans and Squirm went to find the science store. Zo-Zo went off too, but she didn't say where she was going.

Griff blew her nose. She'd had a cold for over a week now.

Robin sat beside Griff and stared at the huge Christmas tree that had been erected in the atrium. Christmas! It was only November! What was she going to give McCoy? It had to be something spectacular, something that would make his jaw drop with awe and appreciation, something that would make him love her forever.

She smiled at herself. That was a tall order. She knew she couldn't make someone like her by giving them something, but still, what *did* make someone like another person? Was it as random as it seemed? Or was she missing something?

There were so many different theories. Some people said, "Absence makes the heart grow fonder." Others said, "Out of sight, out of mind." How was a person to know what to believe? Why wasn't there a rule book she could follow? Over the last few months, she'd tried just about everything. She'd tried dressing up, she'd tried makeup, she'd tried being hard to get. McCoy didn't seem to notice one way or the other. Was that because boys didn't show their feelings like girls did or was he just not interested in her? She wasn't sure.

She thought about her dad. He rarely talked about his feelings. Yet, Robin still had a sense of what he liked and didn't like. He liked Laura, for example. Robin could feel that liking. But sometimes he was matter-of-fact and all business. Did Laura know he cared for her when he was being like that?

Then she thought about Derek. He was living with Zo-Zo's mom, so he must like her, but he didn't treat her as if he did. Obviously, the way a man treated a woman didn't always match the way he felt. But why didn't it? You'd think if you cared about someone, you would treat them well, yet that didn't seem to be so.

She turned to Griff. She had her eyes closed and was leaning back against the mall bench.

"Are you sleeping?"

"Just resting my eyes."

"Can I ask you a question?"

"Always."

"Why does Zo-Zo's mom stay with Derek?"

Griff sat up and pulled an apple from her bag. "She probably didn't know what he was like when she first met him. You can't know much about a person until life shakes them down a bit." She rubbed the apple against her leg until it shined.

Robin yawned. What was it about shopping that was so tiring? "But she must know now."

Griff sneezed and blew her nose. "The problem is, when you like someone, you start getting attached to them. Then it can be hard to let go. Love is a powerful force. It can make you do things you never thought you'd do. It can make you forget about yourself and your own needs."

"I thought it was good to put other people first."

"Not if it means abandoning yourself. You have to take care of yourself first or the relationship doesn't have a chance. Look at Zo-Zo's mom and Derek. She makes him more important than she is. That's a recipe for disaster."

Robin shivered, she wasn't sure why. She was about to ask another question when Zo-Zo appeared with a handful of brochures. Excitedly, she gave one to Robin and one to Griff. "I got some prices on flights to Australia. There's a seat sale on right now!"

Ari joined them and leaned over Robin's shoulders. "Flights? For the great whaling adventure?"

Zo-Zo bounced her head up and down.

"Do you think it's actually going to happen?" Ari brushed a long strand of her honey-coloured hair behind her ear.

"We don't know yet," Griff said.

Zo-Zo crossed her arms and slumped down on the bench.

"For God's sakes, Zo-Zo, cool your jets!"

Zo-Zo grimaced. "I don't know how to cool my jets."

Griff studied her with concern. "Then learn, sweet girl. Learn."

Robin winced. She didn't like it when Griff called anyone else "sweet girl." She wanted that name reserved for her and her alone.

Zo-Zo's face soured. "You don't want to go. Robin doesn't want to go. No one wants to go but me!"

Squirm, who had just arrived back, looked at her with big eyes. "I'd go with you. If it weren't for my big science project —"

Griff sneezed again. "Some of that southern sunshine would do me a lot of good."

"Yeah!" Zo-Zo brightened. "It would cure your cold in, like, seconds."

Squirm squinted as he stared at her. "Your nose looks *huge*."

"It gets big as a balloon when I blow it a lot," Griff said.

Ari giggled. "It always looks big."

Griff gave her a playful cuff, then turned to Zo-Zo. "I *do* want the trip to happen. But there are some things that need to be addressed first. As I said, Finn's court case has to be over, then we have to talk to Gord and your principal at school —"

"The principal will just get our teacher to give us homework," Zo-Zo said. "It's no big deal."

Griff's face became serious. "What about you and your mom, Zo-Zo? I know you're worried about her. Are you sure you want to be so far away?"

Zo-Zo tapped her closed fist against her lip. "My dad keeps telling me that until she gets help, there's nothing I can do."

Robin sympathized. She hadn't been able to do anything when her mother got sick either. It had been brutal.

"It's weird," Zo-Zo said, "but I think it might be easier if I *was* away. Maybe I wouldn't think about her so much. Thinking about her wears me down."

Robin felt a swell of concern fill her chest. She tried to connect with Zo-Zo's eyes, but Zo-Zo refused to look her way. She was still mad.

Griff reached over and patted Zo-Zo's hand. "It must wear you down."

Robin noticed Zo-Zo's flushing. Was she going to cry?

"I think this trip would do us all good," Griff said. "But what about permission, Zo-Zo? Do you have to get your mom's permission to go?"

Zo-Zo shook her head. "My dad has custody and he's already said I can go. He wants me to be his newspaper's first foreign correspondent."

Griff smiled. "And what about you, Robin? I know you're besotted with McCoy just now — but I'm not going on this whale adventure unless you're going as well."

Robin grimaced. *No pressure there*, she thought. The truth was, part of her wanted to go and part of her didn't. How could she explain that?

Zo-Zo spun her head around. "You have to *think* about it?" When Robin didn't reply, Zo-Zo's lips curled in disgust. "He doesn't even like you. He likes Brittany."

"That's not true."

"Then why did he have his arm around Brittany at Caitlyn's party?"

"He didn't."

Zo-Zo pulled out her phone and jabbed her thumbs against various buttons until it produced the photograph she wanted. She held the phone out to Robin.

Robin looked at the phone as if it were a tarantula. She didn't want to touch it. She didn't want to see what was on the screen either. It would be hurtful. That she knew. But if she didn't look, she'd be forever haunted by her imaginings.

She squinted her eyes and opened them just enough to see a bit of the screen. Brittany and McCoy grinned back at her. They had their arms around each other and were grinning into the camera.

Zo-Zo waited for a few moments for the impact of the photo to take effect.

"Still think he's Mr. Innocent?"

Anger exploded through Robin's body.

"What do you think about coming on the trip now?"

The anger blasted up through her throat and out her mouth. She couldn't have stopped it if she'd tried.

"Let's go."

CHAPTER FOURTEEN

Now that Robin was no longer letting her worries about McCoy stop her from going on the whale adventure, things began to move quickly. It was if some floodgate had suddenly opened and Robin was being swept down a rushing river. It was scary and exciting all at once. The power and force of it seemed to wash aside everything that had been in the way.

When they got home from the mall, they all went to Griff's for tea and cookies. Squirm had eaten five or six by the time Griff told him to pass the plate to Robin.

Robin shook her head. She still felt too upset to eat.

There was a soft binging sound from Griff's computer.

"Sounds like you have an email," Squirm said.

Griff wandered over to the computer. "The only person who ever emails me is Finn."

Zo-Zo went rigid. "Is it from Finn?"

Griff nodded.

"What does it say?" Robin asked. She felt almost breathless.

Griff read the email out loud.

"Charges dropped. Leaving Iceland tonight. Arriving in Aussieland tomorrow. Buy your tickets."

Zo-Zo shot her fist into the air and pulled it down in triumph. "Great. Let's book the tickets now." She pulled the brochure about the cheap flights from her pocket and waved it like a victory flag.

"We might as well take advantage of the seat sale," Griff said. She turned to Robin. "You okay with that?"

Robin nodded. If she could have climbed on a plane that very evening, she would have.

Griff stood. "Let me have a quick conversation with Gord. He already knows about the trip, but I want to make sure he's okay with us booking it."

Zo-Zo groaned.

Griff touched her cheek. "Breathe, Zo-Zo, breathe." She went out the door.

Zo-Zo ran over to the computer. "Come on, let's look up stuff on Australia."

Images of kangaroos, dingoes, and platypuses appeared on the screen. Robin stared at them, but her mind was on tilt, still stuck on the picture of McCoy and Brittany.

Griff swept back into the room a few moments later. She was grinning. "We're good to go."

Zo-Zo jumped up and cheered. "I don't think I've ever cried from happiness before." She wiped her eyes on her sleeve. They gathered around the computer and looked at the flight options.

"Oh, no!" Zo-Zo said. "We can't get tickets for a month."

"That's all right," Griff said. "It will take Finn a few weeks to get his crew and everything else organized."

Robin frowned. How was she going to stand seeing McCoy and Brittany together for a whole month? She scanned the list of dates until she found the first available flight.

"The earliest one we can get leaves on Christmas day."

Zo-Zo hooted. "Christmas day. Wow, what a great Christmas present that will be — flying to Australia."

"I guess we can have our family celebrations on Christmas Eve instead of Christmas day," Griff said. "What's the return date on that one, Robin?"

"January twenty-fifth," Robin said. The day before McCoy's birthday.

"So, you two will miss New Year's Eve here as well," Griff said. "You don't mind?"

"Mind?" Zo-Zo repeated. "How could I mind spending New Year's Eve whale watching in Australia!? It doesn't get better than that, right Robin?"

Robin nodded. It would be better than sitting at home wondering which party McCoy and Brittany had gone off to. That would be brutal.

Griff entered all their information.

"Alright," she said. "Shall I press the button? There's no backing out once I do."

Robin stared at the bright, sunshine-yellow "Buy" button.

"Let's do it!" Zo-Zo leapt forward and slammed her open palm against the button, then started dancing around the room.

Robin gulped. It was too late to change her mind now.

The next day at school, instead of going into the cafeteria with McCoy at lunch, Robin and Zo-Zo went to the library and started reading everything they could about Australia and the Southern Ocean.

On the way back to class, McCoy grabbed her arm in the hallway. His big brown eyes were full of concern.

"What's the matter? Why didn't you have lunch with us? I saved you a seat and everything."

Robin hesitated, not knowing what do say. Zo-Zo pulled out her phone and flashed the photograph of him and Brittany.

He stared at it darkly. "It's not what you're thinking."

"Yeah, right," Zo-Zo said, pulling Robin forward.

McCoy stood still as they rushed away. He called after them, "Robin, don't be like this."

Robin twisted her head back to look at him. Seeing the misery on his face gave her a twinge of regret. But it also felt good. For as long as she'd known him, McCoy had called all the shots. Now for the first time, she was calling them. That made her feel strong somehow. After school, she and Zo-Zo went back to the library. Griff came and picked them up later.

"Was McCoy at the shelter?" Robin asked when she got in the car.

"Yes, but I doubt if he'll be back any time soon."

"Why? What happened?"

"Gord told him to stop trying to train Rebel. You know your dad. He thinks wild things should stay wild. McCoy stomped off."

Robin felt a *glunk* in her gut. It would be weird not having McCoy at The Wild Place. But it would also be easier too.

Griff stopped at a street light. "Some things just can't be tamed." She cast a smile at Robin. "That includes some boys."

Robin looked out the window. Tiny ice pellets were making flicking noises against the glass. Had she been trying to tame McCoy? She didn't think so. She just didn't want him putting his arm around other girls — was that so much to ask?

Griff pressed the defrost button on the dash. "I'm not ready for winter, yet."

"It's hot and sunny in Melbourne," Zo-Zo said, checking her phone. "Twenty-six more days and we'll be there."

"Hot and sunny. Sounds good to me," Griff said.

As the weather got colder and winter approached with a more strident step, activities slowed at The Wild Place. Robin only went over to the barn after dinner and usually spent her after-school time with Zo-Zo surfing the Internet and looking up places they wanted to see in Australia. Their travel plans gave them a week in Melbourne before they were going to meet Finn on the boat and they both wanted to make the most of their time there.

"The Naracoorte Caves," Zo-Zo said, reviewing her long list of places to see. "That's at the top of my list. It's got giant fossils and there's a cave there too. You can climb right down into it."

Robin looked at the picture of people crawling through tunnels and dark chambers with their headlamps burning. The idea of being underground in rock and mud like that gave her the creeps.

"I'm going to do that for sure," Zo-Zo said.

Robin sighed. Zo-Zo was always so gung-ho to do everything. It made her feel like a slug sometimes. She leaned back in her chair and wondered what McCoy was doing. Since that time when he'd grabbed her arm in the hall, she hadn't talked to him directly, but she still thought of him all the time.

Did he miss her too? Sometimes she caught him looking at her in the cafeteria where he always sat with Brittany and her friends. And in class, too, she sometimes caught him staring at her from across the room. Zo-Zo sat in front of her now. She just moved her things there one day, leaving McCoy her old desk, which he took without argument.

Robin wanted to talk to McCoy, but she just didn't know what to say. And the longer they were silent, the more dense and impenetrable the silence became. But the truth was, she missed him. She felt as if she were walking around with a hole in her chest. The hole had started after her mother had died and now, with McCoy gone, it seemed larger than ever.

Had she made a mistake? One day, she got up her nerve and asked Griff that very question.

"I don't believe in mistakes," Griff said matter-of-factly. "We do what we do and learn what we learn. That's how people grow and change." She paused for a few minutes, then continued. "I think you just got scared when you saw that picture of McCoy and Brittany. You told yourself he liked her better than you. That was quite an assumption."

Robin nodded. She *had* told herself that.

"That assumption," Griff added, "may not have been true."

Robin flinched. Had she misjudged this entire situation? "What do you mean?"

"I think McCoy liked you a lot. He probably still likes you, but he's just not the kind of boy you can tame. He's probably always going to be hugging other girls. He's just a hugging kind of guy, don't you think? Goodness, he even hugged me a few times, bless him. But it's hard to be with a boy like that. You'd have to have a lot of confidence. And confidence is not always your strong suit." It was true. She didn't have a lot of confidence, especially when it came to McCoy. Otherwise, she wouldn't have always been worried about him when he was around other girls. "And of course, you had Zo-Zo telling you he was not to be trusted — that didn't help."

"McCoy is hanging out with Brittany all the time now."

"That might mean that he likes her a lot," Griff said. "Or, it might mean that he doesn't have anyone else to hang out with now that he doesn't have you. Be careful what thoughts you decide are true."

Robin nodded slowly. Were there more interpretations to this situation with McCoy than she'd imagined? Maybe things weren't quite as black and white as she'd thought. Wanting to find out, she began watching McCoy with different eyes. Yes, he was with Brittany a lot, but Brittany seemed to be leading the way, not him. Was it possible that he didn't like Brittany as much as she'd imagined? This wondering made her legs tingle.

She had to find out before she went away. Given that she was leaving in just under two weeks, she had to do something soon. But what? The answer came immediately.

"I'm going to go to the Christmas Dance," she told Zo-Zo.

She hadn't planned to go. After all, who wanted to watch McCoy and Brittany dancing together? But maybe she was just making assumptions again. She needed to test things out.

"You're going to get back with him, I just know it," Zo-Zo said.

"Not if he likes Brittany the way you say he does," Robin said.

Zo-Zo frowned. "Just don't pull out of the trip, that's all."

"Griff wouldn't let me even if I wanted to," Robin said. Of that she was certain.

The night of the dance was bitterly cold. Robin sat in the truck with Griff, willing it to start, but it wouldn't.

Robin went back inside while Griff put the battery heater on the truck for a bit. When that didn't work, she started to give up all hope of going. Then her dad came back and said he'd drive her in The Wild Place van.

The dance was in the gymnasium. The dance committee, which was composed of Brittany and a few of her friends, had tried to turn the gym into a winter wonderland. White streamers and big tissue paper snowballs and snowflakes had been taped on every surface, but the smell of sneakers and volleyballs pervaded the room anyway.

When Robin arrived with Zo-Zo, Brittany was standing beside McCoy. When she saw Robin, she wrapped her fingers around McCoy's arm. As if to grab him in case he bolted.

When he went over to the punch table to get something to drink, Brittany followed. She obviously wasn't going to let him out of her sight. But she couldn't control his eyes and Robin could feel him looking at her. A few times, she dared to stare back into his big brown eyes. His face brightened and he smiled, huge dimples pooling in his cheeks.

The music started and some girls began to dance, all in a group. Some boys joined in. Brittany pulled McCoy on to the floor and she positioned herself between McCoy and Robin, who was dancing a short distance away, making herself a human barrier between the two of them.

Robin danced and danced. Even though McCoy stayed with Brittany, she got the feeling he wanted to be with her. Was she just imagining things? Then, one of the teachers came into the mosh of dancers and said something to Brittany and she left the dance floor. McCoy moved directly in front of her and leaned in close.

"I heard you're going to Australia...."

Robin stared into his eyes. She felt charged up, as if she'd just put her fingers into a wall socket. She tried to pull her eyes away, but couldn't.

"When?"

She told him the dates. It was overwhelming being this close to him. She kept having to keep her body from falling forward into him. All it wanted was to feel his arms around her.

He grimaced. "You'll be away for Christmas *and* New Year's."

Her skin felt as if it had a thousand sensors on it, sensors that were firing off at his every move.

Someone jostled against her and she was pushed into him, her entire body thudding against his. She blushed and pulled away.

"Sorry," she said.

"I'm not."

Robin blushed again. She was grateful the room was dim. Hopefully, McCoy wouldn't notice.

"But at least you'll be back in time for my party."

Robin nodded. "Your birthday is the twenty-sixth, right?"

"You remembered." He grinned. "My parents are throwing me a big party. I can invite anyone and everyone I want. My mom's hiring a caterer, there's going to be a band —"

"Lucky you," Robin said.

He was silent for a moment.

"Will you come?"

"Maybe," she said.

He gave her a shy look. McCoy, shy? What was he thinking? Then he told her.

"I mean as a date, like. My date."

Robin felt a fluster of emotions. "What about Brittany? I thought the two of you ..." She didn't know what words to use.

He grimaced. "I know. She wants me to be her boyfriend, but I — I don't want to hurt her, so I don't say anything, but I —" A troubled look came across his face. "You won't stop talking to me, will you? Like the last time?"

Robin stared at him incredulously.

"You stopped talking to me because I put my arm around Brittany. For like one second. It didn't mean anything. Anything!"

Robin felt unsteady. As if she were standing on a diving board and trying to decide whether to jump.

"So you promise you'll come to my party?"

She jumped. "I promise."

"You won't let me down?"

She nodded again.

He inched forward and pressed her lips to hers.

CHAPTER
FIFTEEN

Beep, beep, beep.

Robin reached for the alarm, but couldn't find the button to turn it off. As she fumbled to find it, she knocked it off the table and heard it hitting the wooden floor. On and on it beeped: *Australia. Australia. Australia.*

She was flying to Australia today! But, at the moment, she was floating in the warm bubble of a dream and didn't want to leave it.

He was kissing her.

In the dream, the kiss went on longer than it had at the dance. But it was just as sweet. She wanted to remember every aspect of it. There was something so special about feeling that part of him touching that part of her.

"Turn it off!" Ari moaned from the other bed.

"I'm trying to." Robin clicked the light on, reached down, and retrieved the clock. Silence, at last.

The red digits said four-thirty. She had never gotten up this early before. It was still the middle of the night. Yawning, she pulled herself up and leaned against her pillows.

Where was Relentless? Usually, the bottom of her bed was mounded up like a grave, with Relentless burrowed under the covers. Robin could hear Griff downstairs, and guessed that Relentless had heard her too and gone to investigate.

Robin closed her eyes and called her. She'd been experimenting with this lately — calling her dog, not with her voice, but with her mind. Maybe she was just imagining it, but sometimes it seemed to work. Trying it again now, she created a picture in her mind of Relentless, then whispered to her. "Come, girl, come."

She concentrated hard for several minutes.

Soon there was the *click, click, click* of Relentless's paws on the wood floor. Griff was right behind her so Robin wasn't sure if her experiment had worked, but it didn't really matter. She just wanted to spend some time with her dog. She was going to be away from Relentless for what seemed, at the moment, like forever. Relentless jumped up on the bed, laid her head on Robin's lap and gave her a mournful look. Robin could tell she knew something was up.

Griff placed a cup of tea on the night table, then slid her fingers along Robin's forehead.

"Did you sleep at all?"

Robin shook her head.

"Me neither. I don't know anyone who sleeps well the night before a big trip."

Robin found that comforting. Maybe she wasn't such a scaredy-cat after all.

Griff went off and Robin thought about the kiss again. It was her first kiss. Ever. And even though it had happened over two weeks ago now, she'd thought about it so many times that it seemed like yesterday. She was so happy that it had happened. Even more so now that she was going away. Strangely enough, it was making it easier to go. The kiss reassured her that he cared about her. She could replay it in her mind whenever she needed to feel him close.

Robin sipped her tea. It was sweet and milky, just the way she liked it, and the cup warmed her cold hands. Outside, the wind was howling. She could almost feel it blowing in through the cracks around the window. She shivered and pulled the covers well up over her chest. It was freezing in her room.

Soon, the temperature in Ontario would no longer concern her. Although it might be a bit cold once they got to the Southern Ocean, it was summer in Australia and people would be swimming in the ocean, putting on suntan lotion and wearing shorts. As hard as it was to believe, in just over a day, she was going to be one of them. In just over a day, she was going to be on the other side of the world. Would she feel like she was hanging upside down?

Brittany would be glad she was going. Robin was certain of that. Brittany had seen the kiss and given Robin a look of pure hatred. No doubt she would do her best to win McCoy back again. But Robin had the kiss and the promise of being his date at his birthday party. Hopefully, those two things would keep the air in her bubble of hope during the weeks she would be gone. They were going for a month, but at the moment, it felt like a year.

Relentless's legs jerked as if she was running. She had fallen asleep and was dreaming about something. Robin stroked her silky fur until she quietened. Then, knowing she couldn't put off getting up any longer, she pulled back the covers and dressed quickly. Outside, the snow was blowing sideways across the window. Who cared? This was going to be the last day she'd see snow in a long while.

Sleepily, she went down the stairs. She could smell the pine boughs that had been wrapped around the bannister. Some of the fronds prickled the skin on her hands. At the bottom of the stairs was a big bag of scrunched-up Christmas paper amassed from the celebration the night before. Usually Christmas was important to Robin, but this year, because of the trip, it barely mattered to her.

Robin went into the kitchen and sat at the table in front of a large plate of shortbread cookies. Griff offered her a bowl of cereal, but she shook her head. Her stomach wasn't awake yet. She put some of the cookies into her pocket and took her things out to the van. Her father must have started it a few minutes ago because it was warm inside. She propped her backpack up in the back and got in. Relentless jumped in beside her and began licking her cheek. Her tongue felt like wet sandpaper on Robin's smooth skin.

Robin buried her face in her dog's neck. "I'll miss you." She felt her throat swell. She hated goodbyes. She'd said goodbye to her sister and brother last night to avoid this very situation. Luckily for her, they had been so preoccupied with Christmas, the goodbye hadn't been too intense.

"You can bring Relentless if you like," her dad said, getting into the car with Griff. "I could use the company on the way back."

Robin snuggled up with her dog as her dad started the van. The headlights lit up the snowflakes, making them look almost neon white against the backdrop of the dark morning.

Robin thought they looked like a flock of little white birds, swooping in one direction and then another.

It seemed to take them forever to get to Zo-Zo's, but when they did, she was waiting at the window. When she saw them, she stood and waved both her arms over her head. A few moments later, the door opened and she came out, a huge pack on her back.

"That pack's bigger than she is," her father said as he got out of the van to help her with it.

"Gosh, Zo-Zo, you'd think you were going for months," Griff said to her.

"I wanted to be prepared," Zo-Zo said a little breathlessly.

They put the pack in the back and Zo-Zo settled herself beside Robin.

"According to Wikipedia, the climate of Antarctica is the coldest anywhere on earth," Zo-Zo said, smiling at Robin.

Robin was grateful for the smile. Zo-Zo had been upset with her the night of the dance, and had been worried Robin was going to bail out on the trip, but all was well between them now.

"In fact," Zo-Zo said as they started off, "Antarctica has the lowest temperature ever recorded on the surface of the Earth. Minus eighty-nine degrees Celsius."

"Good thing I brought long underwear," Griff said.

Robin closed her eyes. They were going to the Southern Ocean, not Antarctica, anyway. It wasn't going to be *that* cold.

Zo-Zo pulled out her iPad and leaned towards the front seat. "Did you know that Antarctica is covered by a sheet of ice a mile thick?"

"That's a lot of ice," Robin's dad said.

"According to this, that's ninety percent of all the ice in the world," Zo-Zo said. "If that melted," she said, reading on, "the sea would rise by sixty metres."

"How many feet is that?" Griff asked. "I always get confused."

"Almost two hundred," Robin's dad said. "And what does your research tell you about the Southern Ocean?"

"That it's famous for its big winds," Zo-Zo said.

"I remember Finn mentioning that," Griff said.

"With no land mass to slow the wind down, the storms must be ferocious," Robin's dad said.

Robin felt her stomach lurch. She didn't want to hear about storms.

At the airport, Robin gave her dad, then her dog, a fierce hug and followed Griff into the brightly lit building. They found the kiosk for their plane and stood in a long line to check in. Nervously, Robin stared at all the people. Each of them stood beside one or two large suitcases. How did airplanes fly with all that weight? What if it couldn't get into the air? What if it crashed?

By the time they were allowed to board the plane, the morning light was just beginning to sneak into the day. Robin was glad. For some reason it seemed safer to be taking off during the day rather than in the dark of night.

She settled herself into her seat and checked out the audio and video offerings. She felt jittery. Suddenly, the plane began to move and Robin gripped Griff's hand. The plane taxied into position for take-off and then did nothing. What was wrong? Had they discovered a terrorist on the passenger list? Was there something wrong with the take-off equipment? She looked outside the small window. It was still snowing. Was it alright to take off in a snowstorm?

Then, in a roar, the engines fired up and the plane began to charge with great speed down the runway. She squeezed Griff's hand as the nose of the plane lifted into the air. Robin felt her body being pushed against the back of her seat by the force of the plane's forward motion. It was thrilling and scary all at the same time.

The plane climbed and climbed until they were above the clouds, then the plane levelled itself and the seatbelt sign went off. Soon, the flight attendant came around with drinks and a snack.

Robin put on the headphones and tried out the various stations. She turned on a movie and watched it for a while, then switched to videos on her iPod. The flight attendant brought a meal on a little plastic tray. It tasted like boiled rubber.

Robin ate a little of it, then closed her eyes and replayed everything that had happened at the dance once more. She liked going over and over it. It made her feel less worried. Then she slept. After all that, she checked her watch. They weren't even a quarter of the way yet.

The flight went on and on and on. They stopped to refuel somewhere and Robin was glad to stretch. Her mind felt as fuzzy as a mouldy dinner roll. The plane took off again and she felt herself become stiffer with every hour. When the plane finally touched down in Australia, Robin would have cheered if she hadn't been so tired. It had been over twenty hours she'd left home and for most of the journey, she hadn't been able to relax. Being tense was exhausting.

They got off the plane and it was all Robin could do not to kiss the ground. Zo-Zo gave her a high-five. As their palms slapped together, Robin knew it wasn't just celebrating their arrival, they were both promising to leave the past behind and have a good time.

CHAPTER SIXTEEN

They checked into a hotel and Robin lay down without even getting into her pyjamas. She was now fourteen hours ahead of everyone back home. Zo-Zo emailed her dad that they'd arrived safely and Robin was going to email McCoy, but the moment her head touched the pillow, she was asleep.

When she awoke, Zo-Zo and Griff were eager to get sightseeing, so she just showered quickly and joined them. Over the next week, they went to all the places she and Zo-Zo had picked out when they were planning the trip. The one with the fossils was amazing. There were reconstructed replicas of animals that lived millions of years ago. Some were as big as dinosaurs.

"Puts perspective on things," Griff said as she looked up at a giant kangaroo.

"How do you mean?" Robin asked.

"Just goes to show you — global warming or not, everything changes. The weather, plants, animals — nothing stays the same."

Robin thought about that. The only thing she wanted to stay the same was McCoy. To make sure he didn't forget about her, she was emailing him and sending pictures often. So far, he'd only emailed back once. Was everything okay? She hoped so.

She suppressed a yawn and gazed out the bus window. Today was their last day in Melbourne and they were on their way to a nature reserve to see more of Australia's animals. It was hot and Robin was still having trouble keeping her eyes open. With the time difference, day was night and night was day. Everything was upside down and her body just couldn't seem to get used to it. Her brain felt like a fried egg that someone had flipped over and cooked too long. She found it challenging to get it to focus on anything.

Once they got to the nature reserve, they rented bikes and pedalled along a narrow road that wound its way through fields of long blond grasses. Every once in a while Robin saw something bouncing into the air over the tops of the vegetation. A kangaroo? She was intrigued. How could an animal that large bounce like a bunny rabbit?

When they got to a lookout that had some stationary telescopes, she caught a kangaroo in her view and studied it. Its head was a bit like a deer's, but its ears were bigger, and it hopped — not little hops, but big ones. And as it hopped, it seemed to turn the earth into a giant trampoline beneath its feet.

"Wow!" Zo-Zo said, reading from a pamphlet. "Says here that kangaroos can be almost two metres tall. And that they can hop up to 70 kilometres an hour."

"That's quite an accomplishment," Griff said. "Given that some of them are carrying a baby in that little pouch of theirs. Look, there's one by that tree."

Robin stared at the area Griff was pointing at. Then she saw it — a big kangaroo with a baby tucked into a pouch on its belly. It began to move and as it did, the baby bounced along inside the pouch, seemingly unperturbed. How amazing was that?

"The babies stay in there for almost nine months," Griff said, reading the pamphlet over Zo-Zo's shoulder.

Robin was enthralled and could have watched the kangaroos all day, but Zo-Zo wanted to see platypuses and dingoes and Griff wanted to see some koalas, so they rode on.

"There is a reptile section we can view if you want," Griff said, when they stopped to have a cool drink. "Apparently Australia has twenty-one of the world's twenty-five deadliest snakes."

Robin and Zo-Zo both shook their heads. Robin didn't mind snakes, but didn't find them very interesting to watch.

They spent the entire day at the reserve and Robin found every hour fascinating. She couldn't believe how different the animals were in this country. There wasn't enough time to see them all, let alone study them.

"I wish we could go back to the reserve again tomorrow," Robin said to Zo-Zo on the bus on the way back to their hotel.

"Not me," Zo-Zo said. "I want to see the whales."

"It won't be long now," Griff said from her seat across the aisle. "We're due to meet Finn tomorrow."

"Yikes," Robin said. The days were flying by faster than she'd ever imagined.

The next day they packed up and took a taxi to the harbour. There were hundreds of boats there and after wandering around for a while, Griff asked a man wearing mirrored sunglasses for directions. He pointed to a wharf in the distance and they made their way towards it. Robin had seen photographs of the *Sea Serpent* during Finn's whale presentation and remembered the characteristic camouflage painting. When they saw it, Robin felt disappointed.

"It's so small," she cried. On the screen, it had looked so big.

Griff smiled at her. "What were you expecting? One of those gigantic cruise ships?"

Robin wasn't sure what she had expected, but it wasn't this. How could a ship this small be safe? What about the big winds everyone kept talking about? Wouldn't a boat this size get bashed around in big waves? It made her stomach feel queasy just thinking about it.

Suddenly they heard a loud horn and saw Finn standing at the helm of the *Sea Serpent* waving at them. "Welcome!" He grinned down at them, then moved quickly down the steps.

"Finally." He wrapped his arms around Griff and lifted her off her feet.

Griff giggled. "I feel like I'm fifteen again."

You sound fifteen, Robin thought, but didn't say. Why did Griff have to start acting like a teenager the minute Finn was around?

Finn hugged Robin, then Zo-Zo too, and gave them a quick tour of the ship, starting with the helm.

"This is command central," he said. "Where I spend most of my time."

There were windows all along the front and beneath them, a mass of computer screens, phones, dials, and more dials. A man with a beard was standing in front of a large wooden wheel. Finn slapped the man on the back.

"This is my first mate, Roger. If you're nice to him, he might let you steer sometime."

Seeing Robin's alarm, Roger said, "It's okay. Nothing happens very fast on a boat this size. It's not like a go-cart."

They trundled down some metal steps and along a corridor Finn called a "companionway," then he pushed open a door.

"Here's your cabin," he said.

It was a small room with two bunk beds, a small vinyl covered couch, and a tiny desk.

"The Head, or washroom, is two doors down. There's four for all thirty-five of us —"

Robin nodded. The implication was clear. No lingering.

Zo-Zo set down her backpack. "There's no window in here."

"Nope. No portholes on this level. You're under the water-line, so you wouldn't see much anyway. Just black water."

Black water. Robin repeated the words. They sounded ominous somehow.

"Where's Griff going to sleep?" Robin asked.

"She gets to be on the upper deck near me," Finn said. "Given her frail old age, I thought she deserved her own room and her own porthole."

Griff gave him a jocular poke and they moved on.

Robin stuck close to Griff. She wished her grandmother was going to be sleeping closer.

As they went, Finn introduced them to other crew members as they appeared. They were of every age and nationality.

"Everyone on the ship is a volunteer," he explained. "They're here for one reason and one reason alone — they're passionate about whales."

Zo-Zo elbowed Robin. "Animal fanatics, just like us."

Finn took them next to what he called the "mess hall." There were benches and tables like in any dining area, but they were all screwed to the floor.

Robin was about to ask why everything was screwed down, when the realization hit her. The winds. And waves. Of course. She shivered.

"And over there's the galley, or kitchen. Just past that is the scullery, where we do the dishes."

He took them inside the galley where a big burly guy was kneading a large round of dough. He had two piercings, one high up on his ear and the other in the side of his nose, which always made Robin want to sneeze.

"This is Darwin," Finn said.

Darwin's muscular arms continued to work the dough. On one bicep was a tattoo of a pink octopus. "I'd shake your hands but —" He laughed. It was a deep, rich laugh and it filled the galley.

Robin moved her eyes around the kitchen. It looked very much like any other kitchen except for the fact that there were brackets on the shelves and stove. Someone had gone to a lot of trouble to make sure things stayed in place. That made Robin nervous. Were storms that frequent?

"Darwin makes the best sticky buns in the Southern Ocean," Finn said.

"I love sticky buns," Zo-Zo said. She and Darwin grinned at each other.

As they left the kitchen, Zo-Zo leaned close to Robin and whispered.

"Yummy."

"You talking about him or the sticky buns?" Griff asked. Finn roared. Zo-Zo smirked, but made no comment.

CHAPTER
SEVENTEEN

For the next few days, Robin and Zo-Zo pitched in with the rest of the crew loading supplies on board. They carried bags of potatoes and onions, boxes of apples and oranges, crates of vegetables and nuts and seeds. When they weren't busy loading things, they had practise drills, which involved everything from getting the rubber Zodiac boats in and out of the water, to rehearsing fire alarms and practising man-overboard procedures.

Robin found manoeuvring the Zodiacs in and out of the water the hardest skill to master. They had to unclamp the rubber boats, then raise them by a pulley, and if it was windy, which it seemed to be most of the time, the boats would sway and spin. Robin kept expecting one of the boats to hit her in the head, but that never happened.

Luckily, Zo-Zo had managed to get the two of them paired up with Darwin, who was familiar with the Zodiacs from other campaigns and knew how to handle them. At first, they practised the drills while tied up to shore, but one day Finn took the ship just outside the harbour where it was windier and wavier.

Out there, the sky seemed huge. At home, there was always something filling the sky — trees, houses, rocks, buildings — but an hour or so away from shore, as they were now, the sky gaped open like a giant mouth. It frightened her. Her father was right. There would be nothing to slow the winds down out here. She thought about those little rubber toys you could buy that expanded to fifty times their size when you put them in water. The wind would be like that down here, but worse.

Once they were far enough out, Finn cut the engines and put the crew through the various drills once again. As they went through the routines, he watched from the helm, shouting suggestions when they did things wrong and cheering them on when they got things right.

"If you can't do it when the water is calm," Finn called to them through a megaphone, "imagine trying to do it when you're on a roller coaster wave." Robin couldn't imagine it. Didn't want to imagine it.

They went farther out the next day and farther the day after that. But each night, they came back into the harbour. Robin was glad. There was something reassuring about being tied to a dock every night. She liked the idea that she could just get off the boat if she wanted to. Soon that wouldn't be possible. Once they set out to sea, she would be trapped. Her access to "civilization" would not just be hours or days away, it might be as long as a week away. That scared her.

What if she got sick and they were way out at sea? Or what if she had an accident? There was a doctor on board, but what if she needed a hospital? If a person got acute appendicitis, for example, they could die if they didn't get to a hospital.

She wished she didn't have all these worries. Why couldn't she be more like Zo-Zo and just be excited about this adventure? She pulled out a calendar and counted out sixteen days. That's how long they were going to be at sea — eight days to get to the Southern Ocean and eight days to get back. Her reward would be McCoy's party.

When the day came to set out, Robin asked Griff one more time.

"You promise I'll be back for McCoy's party?"

"Absolutely," Griff said, squeezing Robin's shoulders. "Relax."

Robin hated it when people told her to relax. As if she could just turn her anxiety off like a wall switch.

"Come on, let's go up on deck. I want to take it all in," Griff said.

They stood near the front of the boat and Robin could feel the vibration of the ship's engines chugging up through her legs. The crew cast off the ropes and slowly the prow of the *Sea Serpent* sliced through the calm water and began to make its way out into the ocean.

Robin stood beside Zo-Zo, the wind gently tugging her hair away from her scalp. Overhead the sky looked huge, vast and blue, without a cloud in it. She turned and watched as the sharp edges of the buildings in the city became blurred, finally becoming a dull, undifferentiated line in the distance. Already she was a long, long way from home and from McCoy. Now she was going to be even farther away. A glunk of anxiety formed in her gut.

"Isn't it beautiful?" Zo-Zo leaned forward into the breeze, her eyes closed.

Robin looked out over the ocean. There were a few waves, but the water was mostly calm and sparkling in the warm sunshine. Suddenly, a group of dolphins appeared beside them, arcing through the water, their grey backs flashing like silver as the light reflected on their shiny, wet skin.

Robin had never seen real dolphins before and it excited her. They were so beautiful. She and Zo-Zo linked arms as they watched them, best friends once again.

Griff and Finn joined them. She wished McCoy could be there too. He would have loved being on the ship.

Finn's arm shot out as he pointed to a huge bird that was flying alongside.

"That's an albatross," he said, grinning. "You two study the poem 'The Rhyme of The Ancient Mariner' in school yet?"

Robin shook her head.

Finn drew in a deep breath and recited from the poem.

Water, water, everywhere,
And all the boards did shrink;
Water, water, everywhere,
Nor any drop to drink.

Griff clapped and Finn swooped an imaginary hat off his head and bowed. Then he looked out on the vast expanse of water. "You're going to see birds and fish out here that you won't see anywhere else. The Southern Ocean is the last true wilderness left on the planet. That's why I love it so much. By the time you're my age, there won't be anything like it left on the earth, so take it in girls, take it in."

Robin was quiet. Finn was exaggerating, wasn't he? But then she reminded herself of the extinction lists she'd seen. So many species had already gone. Never to reappear on the planet again. This made her feel sad. And angry too. Why were human beings so bent on wrecking nature?

"But, the planet's getting fed up with us humans these days," Finn said. "That's why we're getting all these crazy storms. Who knows, maybe it'll be people who will get wiped out and not the animals and fish. I'd vote for that."

Robin felt herself trip on the words "crazy storms." She knew she shouldn't ask, but she couldn't stop herself. She had to know the worst case scenarios.

"Is it true what they say about the storms here?"

Finn nodded gravely. "All the oceans ram into each other down here, so it's always a bit wild and unpredictable. Like with any crowd, crazy things can happen."

"Have you ever been in a bad storm?" Zo-Zo asked him.

Finn barked out a laugh. "One time, the wind was so bad, it blew the fins right off the fish." He chuckled and shook his head. "That one was *bad!* Not only did I *think* I was going to die, I *wanted* to die. Anything to end the awfulness of it." His eyes widened as if he was seeing a colossal wall of water in front of him. "The waves were monstrous. *Monstrous.* Some were over eighteen metres high."

Robin felt her own eyes widen and fear clenched her throat, making her voice sound as weak as a whisper. "Eighteen metres?"

"Was scary as heck!" He laughed. "But the exciting things in life are always scary as heck."

Zo-Zo whistled. "That's higher than a three-storey house."

"I was sure the ship was going to go bottom's up. Or wash me out to sea," Finn said.

Griff gave Finn a warning look and began rubbing Robin's shoulders. Her voice was soft and reassuring.

"Take it easy, Robin. Don't let that imagination of yours run off with you."

"Storms like that don't usually happen at this time of year," Finn said.

Thank goodness, Robin thought.

"Or didn't," Finn added, "Until global warming started mucking everything up. Now, anything's possible."

"Finn, stop," Griff said.

Finn shrugged. "I'm not saying there will be a storm, but I'm not saying there won't be one either."

That was the moment Robin knew. There would be a storm. And it was going to be a bad one. She knew it as certainly as she knew her own name. As the realization sank in, she felt her bones turning to mush. Like a Popsicle left out in the sun, she felt like a bag of slush and sticks.

"Robin, don't imagine the worst," Griff said. "If there's a storm, we'll weather it." She put her arms around each girl's shoulders. "Come on, let's go down to the kitchen and start dinner. We've got to work for our keep here."

They made their way down the metal steps to the galley. Darwin, who was scattering walnuts over a large sheet of dough, smiled at them. A girl none of them had met before was beside him, watching and sipping tea.

"Hi, I'm Kim," the girl said. "I just flew in yesterday from the Philippines. I worked in the kitchen on the last campaign and signed up again this year."

"Great," Griff said. "Someone who knows the ropes! I was planning to make vegetarian lasagna for dinner, but I wasn't sure how to make it without cheese. I must admit, I'm finding this vegan cooking a bit of a challenge."

While Kim explained how to make the dinner without using any milk products, Darwin put some music on and they all started chopping what seemed like a mountain of zucchini, onions, and peppers.

When the lasagna was made and in the oven, Robin went to her room to email McCoy. It was fun to tell him all that had happened. She liked writing him. It made her miss him less. There was an email from him too, telling her more details about the party. It sounded like it was going to be huge.

Then someone blew a whistle announcing dinner and Robin went back to the mess hall to eat. The room was full of chattering people sitting on benches. She got herself some lasagna and joined Zo-Zo and Darwin at one of the tables. The two of them talked animatedly and Robin felt left out. She looked around to find Griff. Maybe she'd sit with her grandmother.

Griff was across the room, sitting beside Finn. He was holding her hand. Robin flinched. She liked Finn, but wasn't sure she liked him taking over her grandmother like this.

Tears pricked at her eyes. Even though she was in the middle of a throng of people, she felt lonely. To make herself feel better, she tried to remember the kiss McCoy had given her, but the memory felt dim and far away. Almost as if the kiss hadn't happened.

CHAPTER
EIGHTEEN

After dinner, Finn stood up and addressed the group.

"Many of you are old hands at this whale-saving thing, but there are some new people, so I want to explain a few things. I'll make it short and sweet.

"As most of you know, whaling has been going on for centuries, but in the beginning, boats were small and slow, and men only had spears, so not many whales died. But then ships got bigger and someone invented the harpoon gun and everything changed. The oceans became whale-killing fields and now, our friends the whales face extinction."

Roger, the first mate, added, "I read somewhere that the Soviets killed more than two hundred thousand humpbacks before 1980. Almost wiped them out."

Finn nodded. "That's why the International Whaling Commission put a moratorium on whaling down here, but some countries, like Japan, kept killing whales anyway. Thousands of them.

"But before we get into the ugly part, let's do the beautiful part — the whales themselves. Here's what some of them look like." Finn turned off the lights and the room was plunged into darkness. "After all, they're the reason we're here. We'll start with the biggest ones and work our way down."

There was a clicking sound and a picture of a huge whale appeared on the screen. It had a slightly blue tinge.

"It's easy to see why this one is called a blue whale. Not only are they blue, but they're absolutely *huge*. About twenty-five metres long, weighing in around a hundred tonnes. That's about the same weight as fifty trucks."

"Wow," Zo-Zo said.

"Blue whales are the largest animals that have ever lived — even bigger than dinosaurs."

"Yeah, and we all know what happened to the dinosaurs," someone said.

Finn frowned. "Their hearts are about the size of a small car. Big enough for a child to crawl around in."

Robin tried to imagine a little kid doing somersaults in a whale's heart. The whole idea was amazing.

Finn clicked on to another slide. This one showed a mother blue whale and her baby. Some people made soft cooing sounds.

"A baby blue whale can drink fifty gallons of its mother's milk and gain ninety kilograms a day.

"The next whale I'm going to show you is one of the most common whales in the ocean and one of the fastest." He changed slides again. "This is a fin whale. And this next one is the southern right whale."

He clicked on another slide. This one showed a whale with a bulbous head. "It got that name, believe it or not, because it has lots of oil and blubber and was considered the "right" one to kill. But they're easy to kill too, because they don't swim very fast. They weigh about ninety-five tonnes.

"And last, but not least, we come to the famous sperm whale."

Robin stared at the whale. It had a large square head that looked like a sledge hammer.

"Only the male sperm whales are found down here, but they're the ones that dive the deepest. Also, they have teeth, unlike some of the others, that don't."

"Wasn't it a sperm whale that got you started saving whales in the first place?" Zo-Zo asked.

Finn smiled at her. "Don't get me started on that story."

But some members of the crew wanted to hear it. "Tell us," various people cried.

Finn turned on the lights and sat down on a small stool by the screen.

"It was many years ago now," he said. "I was out on the ocean with some friends when we saw this massive ship. I saw a stream of something red spewing out its side."

The word slipped out of Robin's mouth before she could stop it. "Blood?"

"Yup. What we'd come across was a huge butcher boat doing some whaling."

"Was that the Norwegian whaling fleet?" someone asked.

Finn nodded. "There was one big boat, the one that 'processes' the whale, and a few hunting boats with harpoon guns on the front. The guns were painted bright red." He shook his head. "Funny what you remember, but that day is stamped into my brain like a footprint in mud."

His voice became slow and sad.

"By the time we got there, a female sperm whale was lying on her side in a pool of blood. We pulled our boat up and I put my hand out and touched her. I wanted to see if she was alive and whether I could do anything to save her."

He cleared his throat. "I'll never forget the feeling of touching her. Her skin was so warm. Blood was gushing out of the gash in her side and it pulsed over my hands. It was as hot as bath water spurting out of a tap."

"Was she still alive?" Robin asked. Her voice sounded hoarse.

Finn looked at her with soft tenderness.

"No, she wasn't." He sighed. "I remember looking at her, this beautiful whale, and feeling sick. How could anyone want to hurt something so magnificent? It just didn't make sense to me."

Finn cleared his throat again and paused. "Helplessly, we watched as the men on the butcher ship came over and dragged her into its slipway and hauled her up with cables and winches. Then men with knives started to flay her. I could do nothing. I felt as if I was watching a murder."

"You were," someone said quietly.

"But then we saw a pod of seven other sperm whales go by and the killing boats began to chase after them. I knew we had to stop them. So we moved our own boat in between the harpoons and the whales, hoping the Norwegians wouldn't risk taking a shot and killing one of us rather than one of the whales."

Robin dug her thumb into her teeth. It was all she could do not to rip off her fingernail.

"The whales were racing for their lives and we were right behind them, so close I could smell their breath. There was one very large male at the head of the pod and I knew this would be the one they would go for. We were trying to get in position so he couldn't be a target, but then I heard this terrible explosion and saw a harpoon whiz through the air and tear into the male whale's head.

"The whale made the most excruciating cry of pain I've ever heard. That sound will stay with me forever." He was silent for a moment. "But then, he hurled himself up into the air. I thought, 'We're done for. This whale doesn't know we're trying to save him. He's going to think we're the ones trying to kill him.' And I was scared because I'd heard stories of enraged sperm whales cutting whaling boats in half and killing the crew. And we were right beside him."

Finn stared off into space for a moment. Robin wanted to shake the rest of the story out of him she was so anxious to hear it.

"But then he looked at me. It was the look of an ancient, wise being. I could tell that he knew I was trying to save him, not hurt him. But I also knew that he was telling me, pleading with me, to stop this kind of slaughter.

"Then, message delivered, he sank beneath the surface of the sea and disappeared."

There was silence in the room.

"And so he died," Finn said. "But the look he gave me has haunted me ever since. And I vowed right then and there that I would do all I could to stop the senseless slaughter of these magnificent creatures."

He looked around the room, his eyes soft. "So, there you have it. The defining moment of my life. It got me doing what I do — saving whales. And we've made some progress. We've got the moratorium now. It's just too bad that it made an exception for 'research.' It's that loop hole that the Japanese are using to keep killing them."

He flicked off the lights and a picture of a huge ship appeared on the screen. It had the word "Research" printed in large black letters along its side. Just in front of it, a whale lay on its side in the water, a circle of blood around it.

"This is the *Hanta-kira*, the Japanese 'research' ship."

Some people in the group booed loudly.

"What does *hanta-kira* mean?" someone asked.

"Whale killer," Finn said.

"So, of course, we felt it was important to let them know we weren't going to let them do that."

The next slide showed the *Sea Serpent* ramming the side of the *Hanta-kira*. The slide after that showed the *Hanta-kira*'s harpoon gun broken and dangling from the bow of the ship.

A huge cheer arose from the group. Zo-Zo jumped up and clapped.

"Hopefully, they've learned their lesson and won't be back," Finn said.

"So, you don't expect any boat rammings with the Japanese this year?" Kim asked.

Finn shook his head. "Nope. No boat butting this year."

"Too bad," Zo-Zo said.

CHAPTER NINETEEN

As the *Sea Serpent* moved farther south, the weather cooled. When Robin went out on deck now, she needed to wear a jacket. One morning, she saw an iceberg, gigantic and white, and the next day she noticed bits of slushy ice floating in the water. As the days passed, to her great relief, the water stayed calm. Maybe there wasn't going to be a storm after all. Maybe it was just fear trying to get a foothold in her mind. Fear did that sometimes, told you bad things were going to happen and then they didn't.

Every day, the first thing Robin did when she woke up was check the Internet for the weather. This morning when she checked it, she was alarmed to see a storm brewing, but it was far away and wasn't expected to come anywhere near the *Sea Serpent*.

She told herself to relax, grabbed her binoculars and headed up on deck. She was hoping to see a whale. Because of Finn's slide shows, she'd seen many whales on a projector screen, but no real ones yet, and she yearned to see one that lived and breathed.

As usual, there were lots of dolphins to watch. She loved the way they arched out of the water and swam alongside the ship. They seemed to be perpetually smiling, as if they were always happy. But then why wouldn't they be happy? They got to play with their friends in the water all day, every day. She'd be happy if she could do that too.

Yesterday, she'd seen some penguins and seals, but there was nothing like that today. She scanned the surface of the ocean. It was a mass of glittering light — as if all the stars in the universe were playing on the ocean's surface. It was beautiful, but there were no whales in sight.

Determined, she continued to scan the water. She wasn't even sure what she was looking for. A giant fin? A colossal tail? What she wanted most was to see a whale breach. She couldn't imagine how anything that large could throw itself up in the air and she wanted to see it for herself.

After watching for a long time, she had an idea. Maybe she could call a whale in, like she tried to call Relentless to her sometimes. It was worth a try. She shut her eyes and concentrated hard on imagining a whale.

"Come on, whale," she whispered. "I'm waiting for you."

After a while, she opened her eyes again. *Oh well. Nice try.*

She picked up her binoculars and went down to the kitchen to help with lunch. As usual, her mind drifted to McCoy and how the plans were coming for his party. The party was sounding huge. His parents were paying for a band and he'd invited over a hundred kids. It was going to be amazing. And she was going to be his date. It didn't get better than that.

"Whales!" Someone shouted.

Everyone scrambled up on deck, including Robin, Griff, and Zo-Zo.

"There! There!" Zo-Zo pointed, bouncing on her toes.

Robin saw the rim of the whale's long body in the water and smiled. Had she been responsible for the whale coming? She doubted it, but was too enthralled to care. Because she'd seen Finn's pictures and heard him talk about the weight and size of whales, she thought she knew what to expect. Yet still, the colossal size of it made her jaw drop. The whale was gliding in the water a few hundred metres from the boat and she could see the top of it, from tip to tail, just above the water line. Nothing could have prepared her for the size of it. She was flabbergasted.

Zo-Zo's voice was hushed. "Wow — that's bigger than big."

It was. It truly was. Robin couldn't take her eyes off it. The whale slipped farther down in the water and disappeared. *Oh no! Was that it?* Was that all she going to see of it?

Robin scanned the surface around the boat for several minutes and was just about to give up on seeing it again, when the whale hurled itself out of the water, flinging its giant body into the air. It seemed to go up and up and up, then crashed down, making a loud whacking sound as it hit the surface, sending a massive spray of water in every direction.

A few droplets landed on her face. She was tempted to run down to the kitchen and get an empty jar so she could collect the splash water. What a souvenir that would be. Maybe she could give it to McCoy for his birthday. That would be the most unique present ever.

But that would mean leaving the whale and she didn't want to leave the whale, even for a few minutes, so she stayed with the rest of the crew and watched the whale swimming, spouting water, and occasionally breaching or whacking its tail loudly on the surface of the water. She felt mesmerized, mesmerized by its size, mesmerized by the way it moved, mesmerized by ... she was struggling for the right word when she remembered what Finn sometimes said. Yes, she was mesmerized by it "magnificence."

Finn came and stood beside Robin as Zo-Zo took pictures.

"I've seen this whale before," Finn said. "Next time she breaches, take a look at her tail. A small chunk has been torn out of the right side." He bunched his lips into a fist. "That research boat I was telling you about killed her mother last year. It had this one in its sights too until we chased it off."

Robin felt a surge of kinship for the young whale. Both of them had lost their mothers.

"Sad," Finn said, "but at least we saved her."

"They would have killed the mother *and* her baby?" Robin asked. Even in Canada, hunters tried to spare babies.

"To them, whale meat is whale meat." Finn scowled. "That's why we're vegan on the ship here. So people will realize they can eat well without having to kill animals."

Robin nodded. She wasn't minding the vegan diet at all. She was still able to eat burgers, but they were bean burgers, and she could still spread "butter" on her toast, but it was soy butter.

The whale disappeared again, and after a while the crowd of people began to slowly return to their work stations.

"Come on, you pollywogs," Griff said, putting her arms around Robin and Zo-Zo. "Time to get back to work."

"Oh, please can we stay for a little while longer?" Zo-Zo asked. "Just in case the whale comes back?"

"Okay," Griff said. "Darwin's made some sprouted sunflower seed bread and Kim can help me put the sandwiches together. But don't be too long, okay?"

Robin and Zo-Zo nodded and soon they were the only two left on deck.

"There she is again," Robin said. The whale was farther out now, but they could see her with their binoculars. Robin felt a deep sense of awe.

"I bet she knows we're watching her," Robin said.

As if to prove that she was, the whale swam in closer, then breached.

"See? See the nick on her tail?"

Zo-Zo nodded.

The whale breached again.

"Maybe she's trying to tell us something," Robin said. "In whale language."

"Yeah," Zo-Zo said. "Whales are supposed to be really smart. Their brains are like the biggest of any animal on the planet."

The whale whacked her tail on the water.

Robin laughed. "I think she likes that we're calling her smart."

"She sure has a lot of spirit," Zo-Zo said.

She sure did, Robin thought. "I'm going to call her Spirit."

"Cool," Zo-Zo said. "I like that."

They watched Sprit for a while longer.

"It's like she's putting on a show just for us," Robin said.

Zo-Zo kept taking pictures. "I'm going to take a video of her breaching." She tapped some buttons on her phone. "Okay, Spirit. Do your stuff. For everyone back in Canada."

Spirit breached one more time, as if on request, soaring up even higher, then thundering down and finally plunging into the ocean's depths. She didn't reappear again.

Robin rested her arms and chin on the metal railing. She felt a deep sense of contentment. In front of her, the ocean sparkled. It looked as if someone had thrown thousands of sequins all over its surface. A slight breeze wafted across her face, just enough to cool her from the warm sun that was beaming down on her skin. And she'd just seen the most magnificent whale. She couldn't wait to write to McCoy and tell him all about it. It wouldn't be so long until she saw him again. In another three days they'd be changing direction and starting back.

Zo-Zo pulled herself up and Robin followed her down the stairs. As she went, she felt her body pitch ever so slightly to the right. She grabbed the handrail and steadied herself.

Oh-oh.

It's nothing, she told herself. *Probably the swell from another boat.*

But her body didn't believe her. And her body was right.

CHAPTER TWENTY

Robin continued down to the galley and began preparing salad. She cut up some celery, gathered it into her cupped hands, and was just about to drop it into a metal bowl, when the bowl slid away from her. She stood frozen in place, only her eyes moving as the bowl slid away, then slid back again.

Kim began clearing things from the counters and putting what she could into cupboards.

Darwin dipped his head towards Robin. "Hope you like rock 'n' roll."

"I do," Zo-Zo said, overhearing.

Robin didn't trust herself to speak.

Darwin reached into his jeans and pulled out a plastic tube of pills. He tapped a few into his palm and stared at them. "Hmm. Puke yellow. How apt." He popped some in his mouth, then held the tube out to Robin. "You're looking a bit green behind the gills. Want a few? I've got lots."

Robin shook her head. She didn't like the idea of taking pills from someone she barely knew. Besides, she didn't even know if she was going to need them.

According to the Internet, that storm wasn't coming anywhere near where they were. Sure, they might get some of the winds at the edge of it, but so what? She could take a bit of wind, couldn't she? The waves might get bigger for a few hours, but that didn't mean there was anything to worry about. And even if the waves did get bigger, that didn't mean she was going to be seasick. She'd read up about seasickness. Not everyone got it. Even in a storm. And they weren't in a storm. They were in some choppy water. That was all. She was just going to have to wait and see how her body handled it.

She didn't have to wait long.

As they finished preparing for lunch, everything started to rock and sway. The movement was slow at first, utensils shuffling across counters, a few clattering loudly to the floor. Then the hanging pots above the work area started banging into each other.

"Storm music," Darwin said. "Soon, everything's going to dance."

The others laughed. Not Robin.

"I'll get the ginger tea going," Kim said. "Just in case."

"Just in case of what?" Robin asked.

Kim turned to fill the kettle. "Just in case your stomach doesn't like dancing." She and Darwin exchanged a cautious look.

As Kim made the tea, Robin carried a large bowl of salad to the serving area. Suddenly, she was thrown against the cupboards. Darwin lunged towards her and grabbed the bowl before the salad flew out of it.

"I'll take it from here," he said.

Robin nodded and walked with her hand against the wall back into the kitchen.

Within a short period of time, the swaying became continuous. Robin tried bending her knees and moving with it, but it was difficult. Her stomach didn't like the instability one bit.

When it was time to eat, Robin watched the others helping themselves to lunch. Zo-Zo ate both a sandwich and some salad, but Robin had no appetite at all. She felt as if she had a heavy ceramic bowl full of squirming fish careening around in her stomach. Kim gave her some ginger tea and she sipped it slowly, hoping it was going to help.

"Keep your eyes on the horizon," Kim said. So Robin trudged up to the deck where she thought she'd be able to see it better. The water, which had been calm as a mill pond a few hours ago, was now a rollicking mass of rolling swells. Every few moments, one of them smashed into the side of the ship, sending spumes of water high into the air. Afraid, Robin went back downstairs, holding firmly onto the handrails as she went.

When she got to her cabin, she crawled into bed, hoping she would feel more stable there, but she didn't. And now that she was focussing on it, the pitching seemed worse than ever. She tried to distract herself by getting on the computer, then reading, but after a while, she realized they were both just making her feel nauseous, so she stopped. All she could do was wait for the winds to blow themselves out. But the winds got worse and were soon whistling and screaming like some kind of tortured animal.

Finally, she fell into an anxious sleep. When she awoke, the boat was rising and falling in an ominous way. Her heart began to pound. What if the boat capsized? Hundreds of tons of freezing water would come plunging into the ship, drowning them all. Should she go up on deck and get into a life boat? At least then, if the worst happened, she'd be ready. But she'd get soaked out there. Gripped with fear, she remained where she was.

Just before dinner, she heard voices in the hall. Suddenly, Zo-Zo and Darwin fell into the room. They were trying to hold onto each other for support, but like two drunkards, they couldn't get their balance and kept bashing into each other and laughing.

"This is like being in a bumper car at the Ex," Zo-Zo said. "Except there's no brake." She leaned against the far wall and braced her arm against the desk. She looked at Robin with concern. "We came to check on you."

Robin stared at them. How come they weren't sick like she was? How could they be enjoying the very thing that was making her want to throw up?

The boat pitched again and Zo-Zo put her other hand on the bunk bed to steady herself. "You look a bit green."

"I was going to say yellow," Darwin said.

Robin stared at them, willing herself not to cry.

"Mohammed, one of the guys in the engine room, he's seasick too," Zo-Zo said. "He upchucked right in front of us in the companionway."

Robin closed her eyes. She didn't want to think about throwing up. She *hated* throwing up. Absolutely *hated* it.

"Maybe you should try some of Darwin's motion sickness pills," Zo-Zo said. "Give her some Darwin."

Despite the wiggling fish in her stomach, Robin shook her head. "I'll wait till Griff comes. See what she says." Where was Griff anyway? Why hadn't she come to see her?

"We brought you more ginger tea," Zo-Zo said.

Zo-Zo passed her a Thermos and Robin raised it to her lips. Just as she began to drink, the boat lurched and the tea spewed down her front, the hot liquid burning.

Zo-Zo pressed her lips together and handed her a towel.

Robin set the Thermos aside. I'll go and get Griff," Zo-Zo said. She moved towards the door.

"Can you bring me something?" Robin said weakly.

"What?"

"A bucket."

"Poor girl," Griff said when she came in a while later. She turned to Finn, who was behind her. "Should we call the ship's doctor? Isn't there something she can take?"

His weathered face broke into a sympathetic smile. "The best thing to do is just ride it out." He turned his gaze to Robin. "You'll feel better in a few days."

A few days?

"Seasickness is a strange thing," he said. "Some people get it every time they ship out, even in the mildest winds. Other people don't get it, even in a storm. There's no rhyme or reason to it. I've only had it once, so I know how gruesome it is. But believe me, the winds could be a lot worse."

Robin looked at Finn's tanned, calm face. *Worse? No. Please no.* She groaned.

Griff gave Finn a stern look. "Don't scare her any more than she already is."

Robin shut her eyes quickly. It was all too much. If only there was some way of getting off the boat. But there wasn't.

Griff sat on the side of Robin's bed and squeezed her hand. "Don't get yourself in a state, Robin. No matter what happens, we'll get through this." She stood up. "I'm not feeling great myself. But, I have to finish making dinner. I'll come back right after."

Please don't go, Robin wanted to say, but didn't. Couldn't Griff see that she needed her?

When they left, Robin lay back in bed. She tried to sleep again, but couldn't. The boat was pitching even more forcefully now and she held onto the sides of her bunk with stiff arms. Could the boat actually roll over? What if it did? They would all drown.

Robin waited and waited for Griff to come, but she didn't. Where was she? *With Finn,* Robin thought bitterly. *Her new love. She doesn't care about me anymore.*

No one came for hours. When someone finally did arrive, it wasn't Griff, it was Zo-Zo.

"I was waiting for Griff," Robin asked. "But I guess she's with Finn. Her *boyfriend.*"

"Whoa, you sound pissed," Zo-Zo said.

"She's acting *stupid.*"

"It's the same way you act around McCoy."

Robin looked away.

Zo-Zo got into her pyjamas. "I heard the two of them talking about Griff coming on the boat full time."

Robin sat up stiffly. "What? You mean leave The Wild Place?"

Zo-Zo shrugged. "Finn was telling her why she should come and live on the boat with him."

Robin felt furious. How dare Finn try and take Griff away from her. Would Griff even consider that? She wouldn't, would she? No. Robin couldn't imagine it. Griff loved them, loved the animals and The Wild Place — she wouldn't leave them, would she?

Zo-Zo got into bed. In moments, Robin could hear the soft snuffle of her sleeping breath. Robin felt furious. If the two of them had been sleeping on some sandy beach somewhere, she wouldn't have resented it, but they were in a violent storm! Didn't Zo-Zo realize that? How could she sleep in this chaos?

Robin told herself to relax, but couldn't. She wanted to sleep, was desperate to sleep — anything to take her away from her thoughts and the endless tossing and rocking movement of the boat, but sleep was impossible.

All night the winds howled. The boat heaved and pitched and rolled and plunged until Robin thought she was going to go out of her mind. She put on her life jacket and gripped the rails of her bunk bed. Terrified, she followed each roll of the boat, going up and up each roller coaster wave, then crashing down and down until she was certain the boat had gone underwater and the ocean would come bursting through the cabin door. Sometime in the night she threw up, expelling what felt like squirming eels into a bucket. It didn't make her feel any better. She threw up again. And again. It was as if her stomach didn't want to be in her body either.

Zo-Zo snored on, unaware.

Robin must have slept because they next thing she knew, Zo-Zo was sitting on the bottom of her bed. The bucket had been emptied and there was a new Thermos of ginger tea on the desk.

"Griff's sick too," Zo-Zo said. "That's why she didn't come last night. She's throwing up like you are."

"But you aren't," Robin said. That was the part that was unfair.

"So far, so good," Zo-Zo said. "But half the crew is upchucking. Now Darwin is sick too, even though he took those pills. Kim and I have to run the kitchen all by ourselves. I'd better go. I cleaned up your bucket."

Robin knew she should say thank you, but she was too angry. Besides, the room still stank of vomit. The smell of it made her want to throw up again. Robin watched Zo-Zo leave. *Great. She was in this entirely alone.*

The storm went on and on and on. Fear tightened every muscle in her body, widened her eyes, and made her palms sweat. She couldn't sleep, she couldn't read, she couldn't think. All she could do was follow each wave as it pushed the boat up and up, then took the boat down and down. Each time, she was sure the boat would capsize, but it didn't.

At times, she wished it would. Then perhaps, this living hell would be over. Never in her entire life had she felt so miserable.

The only thing that consoled her was the thought of going home. Home. It made her eyes sting just thinking about it. Every day, she made a dark slash through another day on her calendar. If they were going to make it back on time for their flight, and McCoy's party, they needed to turn around tomorrow. Could a boat turn around in a storm? It had to. Somehow, some way, this boat had to start making its way back to Australia tomorrow. Her entire being longed for land, longed for her dog, her dad, her life at home. Every hour that passed, that longing became stronger until every fibre in her body shouted one irrevocable demand: *Home. Home. Get me HOME.*

CHAPTER
TWENTY-ONE

The next day when Robin opened her eyes, she lay perfectly still, listening. It was very early and the dim morning light was barely sneaking into the room. Something was different. There was no whistling wind. And the boat wasn't rocking anymore.

Scrambling out of bed, she pulled on her jacket and boots and wobbled her way up to the deck. Weak and exhausted, she stared out at the ocean. There were waves, but they were small and instead of pushing the boat around, they were just lapping lightly on the side of it. Her legs almost buckled with relief. She felt like crying. The storm was over and they could go home. *HOME!* Finally.

Zo-Zo appeared beside her and the two of them sat on the edge of a life boat.

"We'll be starting back today," Robin said.

"Yeah," Zo-Zo said. She didn't sound anywhere near as excited by this prospect as Robin was.

Robin lifted her binoculars and scanned the surface of the water. Soon she would be seeing land. LAND! She could hardly wait.

There was a mist on the surface of the water, a mist that shifted and swirled as she moved the binoculars. She was looking for Spirit. What did whales do during storms? Did they swim way down underneath where the water was calm or did they play in the gigantic waves? Maybe for whales, storms were fun.

As she moved the binoculars along the horizon, she saw something dark and ominous way in the distance. The mist came up again and she lost sight of it, but she kept staring at the same spot until the mist shifted again.

A ship appeared. A big ship. As she stared at it incredulously, she saw that something was printed on its side. The mist kept appearing and disappearing so it was hard to decipher the printing, but finally she was able to make out the word "search." Was the boat some sort of search vessel? Had someone been lost in the storm? Then she saw two other letters, the ones that went in front of the word "search." The first letter was *R* and the second was *e*.

That spelled "Research."

Robin repeated the word. *Research*.

A torpedo charged through the depths of her, exploding in a realization. Was this the research boat Finn hated so much? The one that had killed hundreds of whales? The one Finn bashed and chased away last year? No, it couldn't be. Finn said it wouldn't be back.

There must be some mistake.

The mist cleared and the entire boat was suddenly visible. There was no mistaking it. No mistaking it at all.

"It's the *Hanta-kira*!" Zo-Zo said excitedly.

Robin stared at Zo-Zo, confusion contorting her face. If the ship was the *Hanta-kira*, why did Zo-Zo sound excited? The *Hanta-kira* killed whales.

Zo-Zo rubbed her palms together. "Finally, some action!"

ACTION? NO WAY! Robin shouted inside herself. They didn't have time for "action." They had to get going. They had to start back.

Zo-Zo stood up. "Finn. We need to tell Finn." She bounded down the stairs, her feet clacking on the metal steps.

Weak and wobbly, Robin followed. She was unsteady in both her mind and body, but one thing was clear; she had to stop them from doing anything but heading home.

Up ahead, she saw Zo-Zo banging on the Captain's door.

By the time Robin caught up with Zo-Zo, the door had opened a crack. Through the narrow opening, she could see Finn. He was wearing white boxer shorts and his hair, dishevelled from sleep, was spiked at the top like a Mohawk.

"It's the Japanese whaling boat," Zo-Zo cried. "It's out there. We saw it."

Finn's eyes became black as a nightmare. "The *Hanta-kira*? Here? No. They wouldn't, they —" He grabbed his binoculars and ran from one porthole to another until he saw it. "Those bastards!"

The door opened wider and Robin caught a glimpse of Griff. She was dressed in a silky nightgown and her unbraided hair was tumbling off her shoulders onto the swell of her chest. Robin rarely saw her grand-mother's hair down and she stared at it like it was an escaped animal.

A possibility hit her like a bucket of cold water. Were Griff and Finn *sleeping* together? No. Griff had been sick. Finn had been taking care of her, that's all. Or was it?

Loud footsteps approached from behind her and Robin turned to see Roger, Finn's first mate, barrelling towards them.

"The *Hanta-kira*!" he said breathlessly. "Eight kilometres starboard. They've seen us and are taking off."

"Let's get after them before they disappear." Finn grabbed a shirt and jerkily pulled it on. "We won't be back when I said we would, but —"

Inside Robin, huge forces churned — her yearning to be home, her need to show up for McCoy's party, the fact that she hadn't slept, hadn't eaten. All these spun together to make one screaming imperative. *She had to get off the ship!*

"No! We have to go back."

The words shot out of her. They seemed to hit Finn like a fist and his head popped back. He stared at her, every feature shouting, *what?*

He tried to push past her to get to the helm.

Crazy with exhaustion and fear, Robin grabbed his arm and stopped him.

Shocked, Finn stared at her as if she were a stranger.

Hating the look in his eyes, Robin turned to Griff.

"You promised!"

Griff's face crumpled with sorrow. She looked from Finn to Robin and back to Finn again.

"I did, Finn. I did. I'm sorry."

Robin turned and ran down the metal steps. A tsunami of emotions roared through her — triumph, guilt, gladness, relief. When she reached her cabin, she slammed the door and threw herself on the bed. This was the worst day or her life.

The door slammed again and Robin could hear someone in the room. She lifted her head just enough to see Zo-Zo standing in the doorway, her chest heaving.

"You're going to risk the lives of the whales for some stupid birthday party?"

Zo-Zo's words splattered against her like mud.

Robin pulled a tissue from the box, wiped her face and blew her nose. Trying to make her voice sound reasonable, even though she knew she was being unreasonable, she said, "Finn can drop us off and go back. It'll only take him a few days. He can help the whales then."

"If there are any left," Zo-Zo fired back.

Robin winced. Right now, The *Hanta-kira* was speeding away and would soon be out of the *Sea Serpent*'s radar. The moment it was, it would be able to go wherever it wanted and kill as many whales as it wanted. Robin dropped her head into the pillow. How could she jeopardize the whales like this? It was wrong. *Wrong.* But she couldn't stop herself. She *had* to get off this ship or she'd go out of her mind.

Neither of them spoke. After a while, it was so quiet, Robin looked up to see if Zo-Zo was still there. Zo-Zo was standing with her arms crossed tightly, staring, her eyes full of loathing.

Robin turned away. Zo-Zo spoke anyway.

"You used to be so courageous. You chained yourself to a barn to save animals, you stood up to the sheriff when he threatened to take them away.... You were strong and fearless and would do anything for wild things. *Anything!*" She paused. "Then you met McCoy and disappeared."

"I did not!"

Zo-Zo continued to hammer home her point. Robin could feel the words pounding into her. "McCoy is all you think about anymore, all you talk about. He's taken over your life."

Robin made her voice sound calm. "Look, I promised I'd go to his party. Promised! He's my friend. I don't want to let him down —"

"Oh, I see. You won't go to the city with me to see my mom a second time, but you'll show up for McCoy, even if that means killing a few innocent whales —"

"But if I don't go —"

Zo-Zo pounced. "If you don't go, what? He'll dump you for Brittany? How can you be with a boy you have to leash like a dog? You deserve better than that."

Robin scrambled for something to throw back. "You're just jealous."

Zo-Zo's chest rose and fell dramatically. "Maybe I was, once. At the beginning. Now all I want is to have the old Robin back. The one who can save these whales. Because right now, she's the only one who can."

She stormed out, the door banging behind her.

Robin grabbed a pillow and sobbed into it. She felt horrible. *Horrible.* She knew what she was doing was wrong, but she couldn't help herself. She *had* to get off this boat, she just *had to.* Sometimes doing the right thing was just not possible.

She was crying so hard, she didn't hear Griff come in, only felt her grandmother's huge hand begin to stroke her back.

"Oh, my sweet girl."

Robin stiffened. Griff would side with Zo-Zo, she knew she would.

"It's alright," Griff whispered. "It's alright."

Robin ran her arm under her nose to clear away some of the drooling snot and hiccupped.

"It's not alright," she said.

Griff pressed a tissue gently into her hand.

Robin blew her nose, then turned her pillow over to get the side that wasn't wet with mucous and tears.

"Everyone on the ship will hate me now. But if I don't go back, McCoy will be mad —" She started to sob again. "I promised him, I —"

Robin began crying again and Griff continued to rub her back.

"It's hard for you, I know," Griff said in a soft voice. "You've already lost someone important. You don't want to lose anyone else."

Robin felt herself relax. Maybe Griff did understand.

"Robin, you have a very special bond with animals. I think you were born with it. Finn was born with it too. The crew all say he can communicate with whales better than anyone. It's a gift. A gift you both have. If you don't go after the *Hanta-kira* today and the whales are jeopardized, you will be severing that bond. Animals will know you aren't trustworthy anymore. Do you want to risk losing that? It's such an important part of who you are."

The image of Griff in Finn's room flashed into her mind. "You're willing to jeopardize The Wild Place. Zo-Zo says you're going to leave and live with Finn."

Griff sighed. "I considered it. Finn and I love each other. But I can't give up my life with you and The Wild Place. Finn wouldn't want me to. So we've decided that I'll spend some time on the boat every year and he'll spend some time at the animal shelter. That way neither of us will have to give up anything."

Robin felt a surge of relief.

Griff slowly pulled herself up and went to the door.

"If McCoy really cares for you, he'll *want* you to stay here and help the whales. Because helping animals is who you are. And if you give up who you are, there won't be much of you left for anyone to care about." Griff went out the door. "Think about that," she said and slipped away.

Robin lay on the bed wondering what to do. Her mind felt as fuzzy as a hunk of mouldy cheese. The air was stale and smelly, so she made her way up the stairs to the deck and tucked herself in behind the Zodiacs where she didn't think anyone would see her. Her nose was plugged and her face felt so bloated, she was sure her head was twice its usual size.

She leaned back and looked up at the sky. It was vast and blue with some wispy clouds overhead. One group of clouds looked like a pair of eyes and a mouth. The mouth was curved downward in a huge frown. Robin cringed. Even the sky disapproved of what she'd done.

She let her glance drift down to the water. There was almost no wind now and the ocean was calm. For the first time in days, she felt her desperation ease. The storm was over. Over. It was time to sort through the emotional debris and get a grip on things again. What a mess she'd gotten herself into.

She thought about McCoy's party. She definitely wanted to be there, but as she relaxed, she could see that missing it would not be the end of the world. There would be other parties. So what was stopping her from telling Finn to go after the whales? That was what she wanted to do, but she couldn't. Something was stopping her. What?

Her body told her the answer. Fear. She was frightened of another storm. She wouldn't be able to handle it. She'd go out of her mind. She pulled her knees to her chest and began to cry again. She was a wuss and would never be anything but a wuss.

She heard a sound and looked up to see Finn. She expected to see anger on his face, but all she could see was sadness. His eyes looked like an ocean of unshed tears.

He put his weathered hand on her head for a moment and Robin closed her eyes, feeling the heat of it pumping down into her body. His hand felt just like Griff's, but stronger. He dropped onto his haunches beside her.

"Glad the storm's over?"

Not trusting herself to speak yet, she nodded.

"Was almost as bad as that one I was telling you about."

Robin remembered. "The one where you said you wanted to die?"

He nodded. "I was sicker than a thousand dogs. For days and days and days. Swore I'd never go out to sea again. But I did go out again. Know why?"

Robin looked into his clear blue eyes.

"It was my love for the whales. That love led me through the fear. Like a lighthouse leads a ship through the rocks. Was as simple as that."

He was quiet for a while. "Life ain't for sissies, that's for sure. But as I've always said, *what just about breaks you, makes you.* I know you're scared. I can feel it. Fear screams through me sometimes too. Still. But I also know you love the whales. Follow that love. It'll make you captain of your own ship. Help you sail any sea, weather any storm."

He made a wide set of pincers with his thumb and forefinger and squeezed his eyes.

Was he crying?

Robin stared at him, not knowing what to say.

He stood up, tousled her hair, and went off.

Robin sat for a long time. Way out in the water, she could hear a whale spouting. Was it Spirit? She couldn't tell. She hoped it was. She didn't want Spirit anywhere near the *Hanta-kira* and its harpoon gun. Just thinking of the gun made her cringe.

She stood up and took a step forward. She loved the whales, there was no question about that. She put her hand on the centre of her chest and concentrated on that feeling of love. As she did, she kept seeing the magnificence of Spirit leaping into the air. Slowly, she could feel her fear ebbing. Then it was gone.

Feeling stronger now, and connected to herself in a whole new way, she walked to the front of the ship and took hold of the sides of the prow.

It was time to put her love into action.

But it's too late, a voice inside her said. *You'll never find the* Hanta-kira *now!*

Robin pushed her fingers through her hair and pressed hard on her skull as if trying to squeeze out an idea. Then one came. Spirit would know where the *Hanta-kira* was. Whales could communicate with each other across hundreds of miles in the ocean. If they could do that, maybe they could find the *Hanta-kira* and lead them to it.

She closed her eyes and created a picture of Spirit in her mind. When she had a clear visual, she whispered, "Take us to the factory boat, Spirit. Show us the way."

Then she raced to tell Finn to start the chase.

CHAPTER
TWENTY-TWO

Day after day, they searched for the *Hanta-kira* and day after day, the research boat eluded them. It simply seemed to have disappeared.

"*Water, water everywhere and not a drop to drink,*" Finn kept repeating.

Robin and Zo-Zo spent so many hours at the front of the ship scanning the water with their binoculars that they started to get red rings around the sockets of their eyes.

"I feel like we're trying to find a spider in a hay field," Griff said, joining them.

"Ten thousand hay fields," Finn said.

Everyone on the boat seemed tense and unhappy as they searched.

Robin worried that the crew members were mad at her for losing site of the *Hanta-kira* in the first place. They had every right to be, she thought. If she hadn't had her hissy fit, they might have found the other ship much earlier.

"They're just worried about the whales," Griff said. "Like we all are."

"Finn will find the boat," Kim said. "He's got a sixth sense about these things. You'll see."

Robin kept visualizing Spirit, kept telling her to guide Finn to the boat. She had no idea if it was working, but she didn't know what else to do.

Then, one day, way in the distance, Robin saw a dark blur on the edge of the horizon. She tensed with hope. Even if it was a ship, the likelihood of it being the *Hanta-kira* was small. But she elbowed Zo-Zo and pointed.

Zo-Zo zeroed in on what Robin was seeing.

"Let's tell Finn," Zo-Zo said, and the two of them ran up to the bridge.

Finn had already seen it and was increasing the speed of the *Sea Serpent,* heading towards what they'd all seen.

"It's probably nothing," Zo-Zo said.

"Yeah," Robin agreed. They had seen other boats in the last few days and each time, Robin had got her hopes up only to have them dashed on the rocks of reality.

Each time, however, Finn had taken the opportunity to radio the other boat and ask if they'd seen the *Hanta-kira*.

No one had.

And each time he'd said, "We'll find that damn boat. You'll see."

But now, as they charged towards the ship they hoped was the *Hanta-kira,* Finn said, "Strange, but I keep imagining that whale I saved last year. It's as if she's been showing me the way."

"You mean Spirit? The whale with a nick in her tail?' Robin asked. She felt excited.

"That's the one," Finn said as he steered the boat closer.

Robin and Zo-Zo stayed on the bridge so they could get the best view. They kept their eyes pressed hard into their binoculars as the boat became more and more distinct.

Robin began to feel a tingling in her legs. That was nearly always a sign that something good was about to happen.

The boat ahead was long and slim, just like the *Hanta-kira*, and it had something painted on its side. Robin couldn't read what that something said, but the fact that there were words at all was promising.

As they got closer, Robin could see something floating in the water behind the boat. Her excitement turned to dread. Was that a whale? She held her breath as it came into view.

It *was* a whale. Lying in a huge circle of water reddened by blood beside the research boat.

"Oh, no! They've already killed one," Zo-Zo cried.

Robin dropped her face into her hands. A whale was dead. Dead. Because of her. It was all she could do not to run down to her bed and pull the covers over her head. She felt so ashamed.

"Don't!" Finn said, his voice firm.

Robin looked up. Finn kept his eyes riveted on the *Hanta-kira*.

"Don't think what you're thinking. Even if we'd gone after them right away, they're faster than we are. They still might have killed a whale before we got to them." He cast her a quick, commanding look. "You've got to focus on the ones you save, not on the ones you don't. Otherwise, you go crazy. Trust me, I know."

His words helped. Slowly she raised her binoculars again and made herself look at the dead whale.

Please don't let it be Spirit. Please. I'll never be able to forgive myself if it's Spirit.

She strained forward, but she couldn't tell. The whale was the same size and type as Spirit, but she needed to see its tail before she could know for sure. *Please no. Please no. Please no.*

Zo-Zo put her binoculars down. "I can't stand to see all the blood."

"Yeah, those huge hearts of theirs really pump it out," Finn said. He picked up the microphone.

"Battle stations. All hands to battle stations."

Griff grabbed both girls by the arm. "You two are staying right here!"

"But we'll miss —"

"You won't miss a thing," Finn said. "In fact, you'll have the best seats in the house. I want you both taking pictures. One on video and one on stills. Grab the camera equipment, it's over there. Come on, get ready."

Finn sped the *Sea Serpent* as fast as it would go towards the *Hanta-kira*. As they got closer, Robin could see that the crew on the Japanese ship were trying to haul the whale up the ramp at the back of the boat. With the dead whale in full view now, she saw that it wasn't Spirit. Tears of relief sprung from her eyes.

Finn charged the *Sea Serpent* closer and closer until the *Hanta-kira* was looming beside them.

He picked up the microphone. "This is the *Sea Serpent*. This is the *Sea Serpent*. We are here to protect the marine life in the Southern Ocean. You have no right to kill whales here. Take your ship back to Japan. I repeat. Take your ship back to Japan. Or suffer the consequences."

The motorized whine of the conveyor belt continued as the *Hanta-kira* hauled the dead whale up the ramp.

"Gosh, I think it's going to rain," Finn said. He nodded to the crew who, at his signal, began fanning out over the deck of the *Sea Serpent* and taking up their battle stations.

Robin looked up at the sky. It was robin egg blue. *Rain?* Then she looked down and saw Darwin and four or five other crew members holding hoses. Suddenly huge sprays of water erupted out of the nozzles and arced high into the air, then cascaded down over the *Hanta-kira*. Robin could hear the water drumming on the metal decks.

The captain of the *Hanta-kira* ran inside and the men working the conveyor belt took off too, leaving the carcass of the whale to slide back down the ramp and into the water.

As the whale disappeared under the surface, Finn nodded sadly. "At least she's back home now. She can rest in peace."

As the body of the whale sunk into the embrace of the ocean, Robin was crying so hard she could barely see what she was filming. Finn stared at the research boat and smiled. "I guess they don't like the rain." He nodded again to the crew, who began loading some canisters into the cannons on deck.

"Hope they like lemon pie."

The cannons fired off like guns. BANG! BANG! BANG!

Robin shifted her camera view to the other ship. Splotches of lemon-yellow goo began to appear on the deck of the *Hanta-kira*. What the heck? The splotches looked bright against the black paint on the boat and began to drool and drip down all over the sides of the ship.

She took a quick glance at Zo-Zo, who was filming the video. Zo-Zo didn't take her attention off what she was filming, but she was grinning.

Canister after canister flew through the air. BANG! BANG! BANG! More and more yellow goo splattered over the decks and sides of the *Hanta-kira*. It was beginning to look more yellow than black.

Robin turned to Finn. "What is that stuff?"

A smile danced around his mouth. "Lemon pie filling."

What? She could hardly believe her ears.

"My cousin used to own a pie company. He went bankrupt and gave me all the lemon pie filling he had. Knew it would come in handy one day."

Robin laughed. She laughed so hard she could hardly hold the camera.

The ramp at the back of the *Hanta-kira* started to go up and the ship began to move forward.

"Now they're going to try and leave the scene of the crime," Finn said. He spoke quietly into the microphone. "Okay, Zodiacs, do your thing."

The crew lowered the two Zodiacs into the water, climbed in and raced forward. Both boats were loaded with huge piles of coiled rope which the crew began to unravel into the water as they shot back and forth across the bow of the *Hanta-kira*.

"Hopefully, that rope will get caught in their propellers and put the *Hanta-kira* out of commission," Finn said.

Robin bit her lip as she took pictures. The Zodiacs were racing just a few feet from the bow of the huge ship. One wrong move and they would be crushed.

The Zodiacs made several more passes in front of the boat and finally the *Hanta-kira* slowed, then came to a stop.

As it did, Finn nudged the *Sea Serpent* in close enough to hit the *Hanta-kira*'s harpoon gun. Robin got a great shot of it being knocked off, then landing in the water and sinking.

The ocean seemed eager to swallow it and make it disappear.

CHAPTER
TWENTY-THREE

As the *Sea Serpent* sped north to Australia, the weather got warmer and warmer. One day, it was so hot, Finn stopped the boat and jumped in the water.

Soon there was wild shrieking and splashing as everyone did the same. Robin stood on the side of the ship wearing a life jacket. She wasn't sure why, but she felt wary of the ocean. Maybe it was because of its vast size, or maybe she just hadn't forgotten the way it had made her so sick during the storm, but she felt a bit uneasy. The life jacket just made her feel a little more protected.

She jumped in and immediately rose to the surface. Between the salt water and the life jacket, she was as buoyant as a cork in water. Realizing how safe she was, she took off the life jacket and lay back, letting herself float.

Under her and around her, in the vast ocean, whales, dolphins, and millions of fish and marine life swam. The ocean and all the life inside it was a world unto itself, but she felt a kinship with it now as if they were all in the same family. That made her smile.

To Spirit and thousands of others, the ocean was home. It took care of them. But as she thought about it, she realized that it took care of way more than its inhabitants, it took care of the whole planet. She wondered if people realized that. Probably not. Like with her lake back in Ontario, it had taken an algae bloom for people to wake up to the fact that their little lake was a living thing that needed to be cared for.

She looked up at the endless blue sky. It was night back in Canada now. Last night had been McCoy's birthday party. Robin had written him days ago explaining about the whales and how she couldn't get back for his party. She'd sent him an e-card yesterday, wising him Happy Birthday, but she had yet to hear from him. She guessed he was upset with her. Maybe so upset that he'd paired up with Brittany — she didn't know. No doubt someone would email her the details later. She was in no hurry to get them.

After a long while, she pulled herself out of the water and joined Griff and Zo-Zo who were sitting on their towels amongst the rest of the crew. Darwin passed around some cake he'd made and everyone was laughing.

Zo-Zo was picking up some phone messages.

"Wow — sounds like McCoy's party was a bit of a bust. There was a big blizzard and the roads were closed, so that band couldn't make it.... Then someone spiked the punch and a couple of kids got sick." She continued reading from her screen. "Apparently Brittany threw up all over McCoy's new, two-hundred-dollar shoes."

Zo-Zo snickered. "I don't think you have to worry about McCoy liking Brittany anymore. Someone's upchuck is a pretty big turn-off."

Robin winced. She could only imagine. She continued to towel-dry her hair. She wanted to hear about the party and didn't want to hear about it all at the same time.

"Personally, I think they deserve each other," Zo-Zo said.

Maybe they did, Robin thought. And if they did end up being together, that wasn't the end of the world. It surprised her to think that. Were her feelings for McCoy not as strong anymore? She wasn't sure. Maybe it was just that her feelings for herself were stronger.

Zo-Zo rubbed her hands gleefully. "Every time he puts on those shoes, he'll think of her puke. It's hard to get that smell out of things."

Robin knew better than most people just how true Zo-Zo's last statement was.

Griff handed Robin a bottle of sunscreen. "Better put some of this on. That sun's hot." She put on a wide-brimmed hat. "I must admit, now that we're heading back, I'm looking forward to being on firm ground again." She took the sunscreen and began to apply it to Robin's back.

Robin closed her eyes. She loved Griff's hands.

"So, Robin?" Griff asked. "Are you still feeling desperate to get back?"

"No," Robin said. She wanted to go back home, but there was no desperation about it. "I'll miss the whales," she said. And she would. Especially Spirit. Spirit had been swimming ahead of the *Sea Serpent* for a few days now, but Robin knew that soon, the two of them would have to say goodbye.

"At least we were able to save some," Griff said. "I'll be proud of that till my dying day."

They lay in the sun for a while, but it was hot and gradually people went back to work. Robin was going to go back to the cabin when she noticed a boat off to the right. She nudged Zo-Zo and pointed. "What's that?"

Griff called over to Finn who raised his binoculars and examined what he was seeing. Finally, he spoke.

"Darn. If it isn't one thing out here it's another."

"Is it another whale-killing boat?" Zo-Zo asked.

Finn shook his head. "Boats like these don't kill whales. At least they don't kill their bodies. Just their spirits."

Confused, Robin picked up her binoculars. The boat was big. Almost as big as the *Hanta-kira*. "If it's not a factory boat, what is it?"

"A 'collecting' boat," Finn said. "They pick up whales and dolphins for marine zoos. See those little buoys out there? They mark what's called 'a purse net.' They set it out, drop in a bunch of little fish into the middle, and when the whales and dolphins swim inside to eat, they tighten the strings and trap everything. Then they pick out the dolphins and whales they want and sell them to marine zoos."

"How horrible," Griff said. "Imagine being able to roam all over the ocean one day, then being thrown in a marine swimming pool the next. It would be like making a person live in a cupboard."

Robin was surveying the boat when suddenly, she saw the sailors running around the decks, slashing the ropes that connected the boat to the nets with long knives.

"They're taking off," Zo-Zo said.

Finn guffawed. "I guess the word's out. *Don't mess with the Sea Serpent.* Ha! Just as well. I didn't feel like doing any boat bashing today."

"There's Spirit!" Robin cried. She was in the middle of the netting purse.

"Those bastards," Finn said. "Leaving all that wildlife jammed into the net. We'll have to cut it open and let them out."

Twenty minutes later, Robin and Zo-Zo were in the water, each carrying a small but very sharp knife. Staying on the outside of the net, they began to hack it apart. The net was sturdier than Robin had imagined and it took a while to make each cut, but slowly, she and Zo-Zo were able to pull the netting apart so the fish could get out.

Spirit, however, did not swim away with the others.

Then Robin saw why. "The net's tangled around her tail."

"Come back to the boat," Griff called. "One swish of that tail and you could get seriously injured."

Robin pretended she didn't hear and swam closer. Right beside the whale now, Spirit was even bigger than Robin had imagined. She was colossal. And beautiful. Completely magnificent.

Using her softest, most reassuring voice, she told Spirit what she was doing.

"I'm going to cut the rope. And free you." She knew she didn't really have to say anything. Spirit knew what she was doing. Spirit trusted her.

When she was done, Spirit began to swim away, but then she turned and swam in a circle around Robin. She came so close that Robin could feel Spirit's body sliding along her own skin.

"You're welcome," Robin whispered as Spirit swam off.

"Wow!" Zo-Zo said, swimming to Robin's side. Together they watched as Spirit headed out to the wider ocean. They bobbed in the water and watched her go. Spirit was free.

Robin and Zo-Zo gave each other a high-five. As if celebrating too, Spirit breached in the distance, her huge body glistening in the sun as she defied gravity and flew into the wild air.

Zo-Zo looked at Robin and they both grinned. Rescue accomplished. Their biggest yet.

ACKNOWLEDGEMENTS

I am truly grateful for the support of so many: Rod Govan, Jason Caddy, Martha Patterson, T. Sansome, Serene Chazan, Linda Wright, Caroline Robertson, Jane Walker, Gaile Hood, Liz Gilbert, Michelle Palmer, and Vicki Govan. I appreciate you all for your unique contribution to my creative life.

Huge thanks to Carrie Gleason, my editor at Dundurn, for her enthusiasm for The Wild Place Adventure Series and for her hawk-eyed editing skills. And to Sylvia McConnell for her belief in me at the start. And Karen McMullin for her promotional savvy and Jim Hatch for always being so helpful.

Lastly, I want to appreciate Paul Watson of the Sea Shepherd organization for his whale-sized courage and perspicacity. He has brought the health of the oceans and their inhabitants into world awareness and put his life on the line to protect them. Thanks to crewmembers Michelle Mossfield and Haans Silver for letting me interview them and learn about life during a whale-saving campaign.

Although the details of the campaigns in this book were catalyzed from research I did on Paul Watson's work, they were created from my imagination.

MEET THE AUTHOR

Hi,

I'm Karen Hood-Caddy and I write The Wild Place Adventure series. I get excited about helping kids take on environmental issues. That's why each one of my books in The Wild Place Adventure Series shows the main characters saving threatened animals or winning some environmental cause.

When I visit schools and libraries I give a presentation called "Earth Heroes" to help kids like you identify their own environmental dreams and make plans to implement them. Visit my website, www.karenhoodcaddy.com, to learn about real-life kid heroes just like Robin and her friends, and to find out what you can do to help animals and the environment.

I would love to hear from you.
Contact me at karen@karenhoodcaddy.com,
and follow me on Twitter @khcaddy

The Wild Place
Adventure Series

Robin Green loves animals, and she'll do anything to save them … even if it sometimes means getting into trouble.

Shortlisted for the CLA Book of the Year for Children and the IODE Violet Downey Award

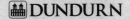